My New Crush Gave to Me

Shani Petroff

Swoon Reads

New York

A SWOON READS BOOK

An imprint of Feiwel and Friends and Macmillan Publishing Group, LLC

175 Fifth Avenue, New York, NY 10010

MY NEW CRUSH GAVE TO ME. Copyright © 2017 by Shani Petroff. All rights reserved.
Printed in the United States of America.

Our books may be purchased in bulk for promotional, educational, or business use.
Please contact your local bookseller or the Macmillan Corporate and Premium Sales
Department at (800) 221-7945 ext. 5442 or by e-mail at
MacmillanSpecialMarkets@macmillan.com.

Library of Congress Cataloging-in-Publication Data is available.
ISBN 978-1-250-13032-7 (trade paperback) / ISBN 978-1-250-13051-8 (ebook)

Book design by Liz Dresner

First edition, 2017

10 9 8 7 6 5 4 3 2 1

swoonreads.com

33614080525644

For Lauren Scobell and Holly West,
who really wanted a Christmas book.
You're not only amazing advisers and colleagues
but also people I am lucky to call friends.

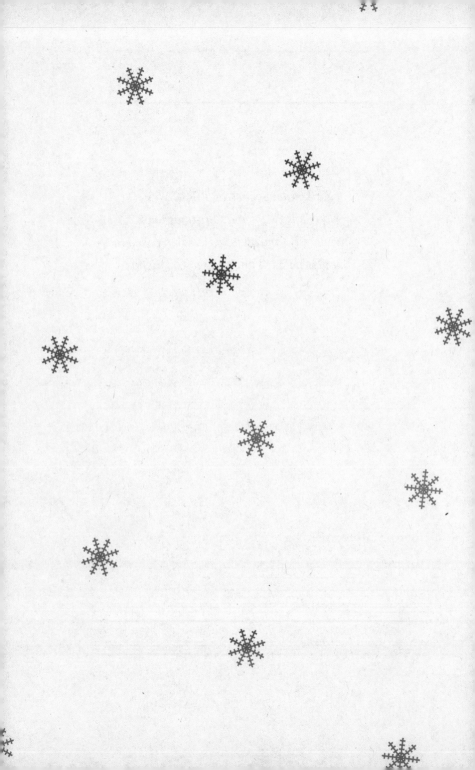

One

Did you get yours yet?" my best friend, Morgan Levine, asked, waving the gaudiest invitation I'd ever seen. It was a total glitter-splosion. An ornament-shaped invitation with enough red, green, and gold glitter to cause shortages at art stores around the globe. And that's not even getting into the velvet lettering and the rhinestones.

I let out a sigh. "Yeah, I got it."

"Why aren't you more excited?" she practically screamed as we made our way down the hall from our locker to the computer lab. "You love this party. I love this party. *Everybody* loves this party."

"Everybody *used* to love this party," I corrected her. For as long as I could remember, Noelle Hawkins held a giant party on December 26th, and it was always way over the top. Her parents owned a lavish banquet hall in town that only the ultra wealthy could afford to book, and every year on the day after Christmas it was all Noelle's. She was born on December 25th, which meant, obviously, that the day was about a lot more than just her. But she hated that her birthday got overshadowed (which I could relate to, since I was born on January 1st). So, in order to make sure their only daughter's birthday didn't go unnoticed, the Hawkinses went all out the day after. One year it was a carnival. Another, an indoor winter wonderland that made the movie *Frozen* look dull. The past couple of years it's been the Christmas Birthday Ball: A Holiday Extravaganza. Noelle's words—not mine. An elegant event complete with snowflake ice sculptures, enough twinkly lights to power a small city, and food that would make the judges on *Top Chef* salivate.

Only this year Noelle decided to go in another direction—the romance route. Ever since Lee Ampuero declared his love for her during summer vacation, everything became couple this and couple that. The invitation even called the party the Lovers' Ball. As if that wasn't bad enough, the other day she told me dates were essential. She was going to have all these little tables for two, mistletoe over every square foot of the place, and slow songs galore.

"It's going to be awful," I said, picking up my pace.

"Oh, come on," Morgan said, matching my stride. "You still talk about that chocolate fountain Noelle had last year."

"Well, they did it with Nutella," I objected. "That's impressive. I can love chocolaty-hazelnut goodness and hate a party."

Morgan stopped walking and crossed her arms over her chest. "Charlotte Donovan, please tell me this is not about Ajay."

She always called me Charlotte instead of Charlie when she was trying to make a point. She got that from my mother.

I turned to face her. "It's not entirely about him." Ajay Das went with me to Noelle's party last year—and he was supposed to go with me again. But there was no way that was happening now. Ajay and I had gone out for thirteen months and twelve days before he dumped me, but who's counting? We met at a program that was basically summer school for kids who wanted to keep learning, even over vacation. But he broke things off this past August. He was starting Yale, and even though the university was only thirty minutes from where I lived (closer than our actual houses), he said he didn't want to start college with a girlfriend. We managed to stay friends. Sort of. At least, he promised he'd still go with me to Noelle's party. That is, until last week when he informed me that he had a new girlfriend, and she wasn't comfortable with him spending time with me, so he was backing out.

Morgan waited for me to continue.

"It's just . . . you know Noelle. She's laying it on about the date stuff and how important it is. And now I have no one to go with."

"You have me," she said.

"You know what I mean."

I started walking, and Morgan followed. "Charlie, you know you don't have to have a date to have fun."

That was easy for her to say. She had a boyfriend. Ira Weitz, and they had been a couple pretty much since Morgan moved to town five years ago. "Maybe for most things, but not this party. It will just be one big reminder that Ajay didn't want me."

"You didn't really want him, either."

"I did, too."

Morgan pursed her lips. I knew she was biting her tongue.

3

We'd been over this about six trillion times. Despite my protestations that Ajay was perfect for me (I mean come on, he was cute, ridiculously smart, *and* a planner), Morgan claimed I only liked him on paper and that I didn't have true feelings for him. But she was wrong. Just because a girl doesn't break down into a weepy mess when a guy ends things doesn't mean she didn't like him. It just means she's able to rationalize what happened and get her emotions in check.

"Even if you're right," I told her, "which you're not, this party is going to be the longest night of my life if I go alone. And you know Zakiyah is never going to let me live it down." Zakiyah Armstead was the gossip columnist for the school paper. She was amazing when it came to finding out dirt on people. She also hated me. It probably wasn't helping my situation that when she'd made a snide comment to me about Ajay finally getting rid of me for good (and that she couldn't blame him), I lied and said Ajay and I were in a great place—and that she could enjoy the lonely losers' table at Noelle's while I danced the night away with my date. It wasn't one of my finest moments, but she caught me less than twenty-four hours after Ajay broke up with me, and I still hadn't fully processed my plans blowing up in my face.

"Who cares about Zakiyah? You two have been butting heads forever. You never let her get to you this bad before."

"It's just everything. I know I don't need a boyfriend, or even a date, I just . . . want one." I pretended to look through my papers as we continued on. This was the best time of year to be a couple. The snow, the cold, Christmas, New Year's Eve, my birthday. And with Morgan spending so much time with Ira lately and my mom taking on more hours at the hospital, I just thought it would have been nice to have someone special to spend the holidays—and Noelle's party—with. "It doesn't matter. It's not like I have time for a boyfriend anyway."

"Hey," she said, sensing my mood like she always did, "if anyone can juggle it, it's you." She elbowed me lightly. "Just add 'new guy' to your calendar. You can fit him in between 7:15 p.m. snack break and 7:33 p.m. newspaper layout design."

I laughed and shook my head, my long titian braid swatting me in the face. "I'm not that bad."

"Right," she said. "And tell me again why we couldn't stop at the vending machine to grab a drink?"

"Okay, fine," I relented. "I like to be on time. I like schedules." That may have been a slight understatement. I had my whole day planned out on my phone, which I synced to the calendar on my iPad and computer and then printed out as a hard copy every day. I even allocated time for "unplanned holdups." It may have been a smidge obsessive, but it kept me focused and made me much more productive.

"So let's schedule you time to find a guy. We have four weeks before the party," she said, her brown eyes lighting up. "This will be fun. A boyfriend by Christmas. It can be like one of those holiday Hallmark movies! We can call it *Countdown to Christmas* or *Jingle All the Way to Noelle's Christmas Ball* or *All I Want for Christmas Is a Boyfriend*. Wait, wait, wait, wait. I got it. *The Twelve Guys of Christmas!*"

Morgan loved holidays. All holidays. *And* cheesy TV. She couldn't get enough of either.

5

"Try more like *A Christmas Miracle*," I said. "There aren't twelve guys for me. If I could find even one in the whole junior class, I'd be shocked. Believe me, I've looked. There's no one."

"That's not true," she objected. "Sean McGinn."

"Flunking physics."

"Gus Janas."

"Can't differentiate between *their*, *there*, and *they're*," I shot back.

"Todd Murphy," she said.

"Didn't know Canada was part of North America."

"Jason Sohn," she tried.

"Late to first period at least twice a week and is always finishing his homework from the night before during class."

"Charlie!" Morgan threw up her hands. "People make mistakes. No one is perfect."

Well, Ajay was pretty close. He had it all. The Seans, Guses, Todds, and Jasons of the world were fine to talk to in school, but not to date. Not for me. I wanted someone that wowed me.

Morgan and I neared the computer lab for our school paper meeting. We coedited the *Sandbrook High Sentinel* (four print editions and weekly online updates). As we were about to go inside, someone came barreling down the hall.

"Watch it," Morgan yelled out.

But it was too late. Teo Ortiz ran right into me, knocking all of my papers to the ground.

"Whoa," he said, and I almost laughed at the stunned expression on his face. He bent down to help me pick up my stuff. "I didn't see you there."

"Sorry," I said.

"Why are you apologizing?" Morgan asked, her voice rising. "He bumped into you, not the other way around."

Teo gave me a sheepish grin and handed me a pile of my papers. "She's right. I'm really sorry. Was mid-text and wasn't watching where I was going. I was just in a rush to get out of here. I hate being late."

"Me, too," I said as we both stood back up. He hadn't broken eye contact with me, and I felt a little light-headed. I had never been this close to Teo before. *Wow, he was good-looking.* Short dark hair, the same color as his deep-set eyes, those lashes that stretched to eternity, square jaw, full lips, and that V-shaped torso with muscles you could see even though he was wearing a sweater. Not to mention, he acted like a gentleman helping me gather my things *and* he was into being on time. There was a distinct possibility he was perfect. "I'm Charlie."

"Teo," he answered. "I should get going, or I really am going to be late. Sorry again about before." He gave me another one of those smiles of his and jogged the rest of the way down the hall.

I was starting to get that wow feeling.

"Do you know who that is?" I asked Morgan, once he was out of hearing range. "That's *Teo Ortiz.*"

"Yeah, so?" she said.

"So?" I tried not to shriek. "You're the one who wants to turn my life into a TV movie, and you don't realize I just had my meet-cute!" Meet-cutes were where a future couple "meets" for the first time in a "cute" way in TV shows and movies. What was better than literally bumping into the guy/girl of your dreams? "I can't

7

believe I didn't think of Teo before. I was so focused on the guys from our class, when I should have been focusing on the seniors. Teo's going to be valedictorian, and he's the quarterback of the football team. He's never had a losing game, he's in the National Honor Society, *and* he plays chess."

"Since when do you play chess?" she asked.

"You're missing the point." I twisted my braid through my fingers. "Teo is perfect. *He's* the one. I can feel it. I hope he's not seeing someone. A guy like that is bound to have a girlfriend. Right?"

"Charlie . . ."

"What? Why are you getting that voice? I'm finally excited about somebody."

"But that somebody is *Teo*."

"And . . ."

We entered the computer lab. No one else had arrived yet, but they still had a little time. Classes ended only a few minutes ago. "Don't you think he's a little 'all about Teo'?" she asked.

"Why? Because he didn't say sorry first?"

"First? You shouldn't have had to say it all!" she objected.

"Okay, fine, but I did. That's not his fault." I sat down and powered up the computer. "And yes, I know some people think he's self-absorbed, but people say that about me, too. And you. They say it about everyone who's focused on a goal and works hard to make it a reality. It doesn't mean it's true. You are the least self-centered person I know."

"Maybe," she conceded.

"Definitely," I told her. "Now are you going to help me win him over or not?" I hoped my excitement would transfer to her.

She looked at me for a moment and then broke into a broad smile. "Like I'd let you do this by yourself? Of course I'm going to help you," she said and logged into the computer next to me, pulling up Teo's GroupIt page.

I clapped my hands together. "I knew you would. Now tell me everything you know about him."

"Not much more than you do. Did you know he's J.D. Ortiz's cousin?"

"What? NO!" I tried not to cringe. J.D. was the photographer for the *Sentinel*, and he drove me crazy. He was always trying to be artsy instead of getting the shots I needed him to get, and he acted like deadlines were suggestions instead of actual deadlines. I could only handle him in small doses, so he primarily worked with Morgan. It helped that they were neighbors. I couldn't believe someone like J.D. was related to someone like Teo.

"He is," she said, and then pointed to the computer screen. "Hey, look. Teo's relationship status says single!"

"Yes!" I said, and looked over on her screen. "Wait? Does that say *Sandbrook High Sentinel* under activities?"

"It does, but I don't remember him doing anything for us. Do you?"

"No," I answered.

"Well, what are you waiting for?" she asked, her voice perking up. "Pull up the archives."

I did as instructed. And there they were—my way of getting closer to Teo—four articles that he had written last year. Teo was part of the paper. This I could work with.

Two

That's pretty much it for the business side of things," Morgan said to the group seated in front of us. "Anyone have anything else before we move on?" Morgan and I were editors in chief of the paper, and we met biweekly with the heads of each section. We had already gone over the number of hits we received on last week's online stories, assignments for next week, and the big holiday print edition.

"I do," Zakiyah said. "I want extra time for my column, just in case there's any last-minute gossip about who's going with who to Noelle's party. Or who winds up *all alone*. You know what I mean, right, Charlie?"

Unfortunately I did, and I was regretting not putting up a bigger fight to keep Zakiyah out of my meeting. She wasn't supposed to be there because she wasn't an editor, but she popped in whenever she wanted a ride home from Katie Boon, the head of features. And Morgan always insisted we keep the peace and let her stay.

"Your deadline is the same as everyone else's," I said. "Unless, of course, you don't want to be in the issue. That can be arranged."

"Okay," Morgan interjected before Zakiyah could respond. "Is that it?" she asked, turning toward me.

"Actually no." I had one more idea that had been percolating since I found out Mr. Right used to be involved with the *Sentinel*. "Next week is the big football game against Laurelwood. We should get the quarterback to do a firsthand report, make it more relatable. I think he wrote for the paper last year. What's his name? Tom, Taye . . . ?" I asked, playing dumb.

"Teo," J.D. Ortiz said, sauntering into the room like it didn't matter that he had missed the majority of the meeting.

"You're late," I told him.

"You are correct," he said and winked at me. Then he flipped a chair around and sat on it with his arms resting on the back. He was so completely smug. He obviously thought the paper was a joke. He hadn't been on time for one meeting all year, he didn't take direction or critiques well, and he always wanted to do his own thing. But there wasn't much I could do about it. Firing him wasn't an option. It wasn't like there was a line of people waiting to be photo editor, and Morgan seemed to have a soft spot for him. So I had no choice but to just deal.

"*Anyway*," I continued and directed my attention to Bobby Williams, the sports editor. "Do you think you can reach out to Teo and get him involved?"

"Sure," he said.

"Great. Then I guess we're all set for today."

"Not so fast," Morgan interjected and stood up. "The holidays are almost here, and I think we need to celebrate!"

I tried to subdue a groan, but it managed to escape anyway. Christmas was a month away, and with everything going on I was already holidayed out.

If Morgan heard me, she chose to ignore it. "We need a party. We can do it right before vacation, the day the paper comes out. What do you say? We can all bring stuff in. It'll be the perfect way to end the marking period." When she didn't get any reaction, she added, "I'll be baking, and I'm taking requests."

"In that case, count me in," Bobby said.

I guess I couldn't blame him. Morgan did make killer desserts. It was pretty much the only reason we got such big turnouts at our monthly full-staff meetings. She tempted everyone with her unique chocolaty creations.

"And we should do a Secret Santa," she said. "How fun would that be, to get cute little surprises leading up to Christmas? And then we can do the big gift and reveal at the party."

"How much is this going to cost?" I asked.

"Yeah," Katie said. "I don't want to spend a fortune on this."

Morgan crossed her arms. "You guys are such Scrooges. It doesn't have to be expensive. You can write a nice note, decorate their locker, things like that. It's about the holiday spirit, not money. Come on!"

I suppressed another groan, but I could tell how important this was to Morgan. "Fine, I'll do it."

"Me, too," J.D. said. "I haven't done a Secret Santa in years."

"Seeing how that's probably how long it will take you to get around to buying a gift, that's probably a good thing," I mumbled.

It didn't go unnoticed. "I'll have you know I'm an awesome Secret Santa," J.D. informed me, his eyes looking straight into mine.

"Just like you're awesome about getting to meetings on time?" I asked. I met his gaze and didn't let go. If it was a staring contest he wanted, then fine. But he had better be prepared to lose.

"One has nothing to do with the other."

"Riiiiight," I said. "Because someone totally irresponsible doesn't let that bleed into all other aspects of his life."

"Funny how someone who is such a perfectionist is wrong so often," he said and gave me a lopsided grin that showed off a giant dimple on his left cheek. And to think I used to find dimples cute. Just another thing on a long list that J.D. Ortiz had to go and ruin. "Must be hard for you, huh?" he continued.

"Me?" I asked. "If I'm so wrong all the time, then how come we almost didn't make print last edition?"

"Because *someone* didn't realize that editor in chief doesn't mean dictator."

"Seriously," Zakiyah jumped in.

Great, now I had both of them to deal with. "No, it means chief," I explained. "As in, *in charge*. As in, I have the final say on what makes the paper, not the gossip columnist and not the photo editor."

J.D.'s whole body stiffened. "You really are—"

I didn't get to find out what I was because Morgan interrupted us. "Okay, this is about Christmas cheer, not Christmas fighting.

You can hash it out after the meeting. Everyone else cool with the Secret Santa and the party?"

Everyone nodded. Although I think they were more excited about the meeting ending than about a group get-together.

"Great," Morgan said. "I'll send out an e-mail. Make sure everyone on your team knows about it and comes to the full-staff meeting Friday. We'll pick names for the Secret Santa then. And editors, I know we usually skip our Wednesday meeting the week we have the monthly staff one, but if we can meet really quickly after school Wednesday just to touch base and make sure we're all still on the same page, that would be great."

"Yes," I agreed, before anyone grumbled at the request. "And, Bobby, don't forget what we talked about. We really want that Teo article, and we need to know if he'll do it ASAP. Invite him to the staff meeting, too. We want him to feel welcome, to feel part of the team." And most of all, to feel like fate helped him find the girl of his dreams, the coeditor of the paper.

Bobby nodded as he made his way to the door. Everyone filed out except Morgan—*and J.D.*—who just sat there staring at me.

Great. I glanced at my phone. *He better not make me late.* I was going to the hospital to grab a quick coffee with my mom. We had barely seen each other in the past three days. Her promotion to chief resident was a mixed blessing. It was great for her career, but it also came with a lot more work and hours on the job. I wasn't about to give up time with her for a guy who drove me crazy.

"*What?*" I asked.

"Are we going to talk about the photos?" he challenged me.

Morgan slunk down in one of the chairs. She knew an argument was brewing. She'd heard it all before. Numerous times. And she always tried to duck her way out of it.

"There's nothing to talk about," I said, gathering all of my papers together. "It's the same as always. Turn in what you have to Morgan, tell her your preferences, and she and I will discuss it and get back to you."

"You know what I'm talking about. I want a spread in the print edition."

Here we go again. "I already told you *no*. There's no room for it."

"And I told *you* that makes no sense. There's no set number of pages. Add a few more."

Of course he didn't care that I had already spent hours doing mock-ups of exactly how everything would fit. "It doesn't work like that."

"Funny," he said, standing up. "You had no problem finding room to randomly add something from Teo."

"I, um, that's going to the part of the paper already dedicated to sports." Although that wasn't entirely true. I was going to have to rework things to make the space.

He crossed his arms. "Yeah, right."

There was something about his tone that set me off. "Think what you want, but this isn't your call. And if you wanted me to take you seriously, you wouldn't have waited until just a few days ago to ask. Besides, aren't you forgetting that this is *the newspaper*? It's not the *yearbook* or some *photography magazine*. The photos are supposed to highlight the news, *not* replace it."

"Wait." J.D.'s hands shot up to his temples. "You're telling me you don't think a picture can tell a story all on its own? Where have you been? One image can capture everything you need—the visceral feelings, the heart of what you're trying to create. How can you not see that?"

I gripped my papers to my chest. "Well, if one picture can show all of that, then you don't need a spread, now do you?"

He let out a snort. "You are too much. You don't care that I'm right, that a photo spread would make the paper better, that more people would want to pick it up and look at it. You're just digging your heels in because if it's my idea and not yours, then it must be a bad one."

"You said it, not me," I countered.

He shook his head. "Morgan, I know she's your friend and you're always defending her, but she's wrong. I deserve this spread. If for nothing else than for putting up with her for all these months. You're editor, too. What do you think?"

Morgan looked from me to J.D. and back again.

J.D. grabbed the back of his neck and rubbed it. As Morgan was about to speak, he put up his hand. "It's okay, you don't have to answer. I'm not going to put you in a spot to go up against your best friend." Then he turned to me. "But I really wish you'd come to your senses."

Then he just grabbed his stuff and left.

"He's so frustrating," I moaned.

Morgan shrugged her shoulder. "He may have a point. We're going to have to change things anyway for Teo's piece. A pictorial spread looking back over the first half of the year could be nice."

"Please, no," I begged. "That will be a ginormous amount of work. One more article is not the same as adding a whole extra page or two. If he had brought it up a week or two before Thanksgiving maybe, but now? I don't want to rejigger everything for this. My month has been stressful enough. But if you really want to . . ." I let my voice trail off.

Morgan relented. "Okay, we can leave it as is."

"Thank you." I really was grateful. I just wanted to go see my mom. The last thing I needed was more work and aggravation because of J.D. Ortiz. I had more important things to worry about—like snagging a date with his cousin.

Three

I got to the hospital with five minutes to spare. I grabbed Mom and me a coffee and took a table in the corner. My cup was empty and hers was ice cold by the time she finally showed up.

"Honey, I am so sorry I'm late," my mother said as she approached our table. She kissed the top of my head. "I tried to get away sooner, but a car wreck came in. It was all hands on deck."

I took a deep breath. Lateness was my *biggest* pet peeve, but it wasn't like I could be mad at her. She was saving people's lives. I had no choice but to be okay with it. "It's fine. Everyone all right?"

She took a seat. "For now. Just promise me you will never text and drive."

I rolled my eyes. "You know I wouldn't."

"I know. I'm sorry. You know how I get." Ever since my mom

started spending more time in the ER, she had become a walking PSA. "So tell me about your day. I miss you. I miss our talks."

I missed her, too. We filled each other in on everything we'd been up to, and the time flew. Before I knew it, it was time for her to go. "Sorry, sweetie, I do have to get back to the ER. There's leftover Chinese in the fridge, and I'll call you tonight before you go to bed."

"Mom?" I said, bracing myself as she stood up. "Any word on Christmas?"

She sat back down.

I knew what that meant.

"I'll be home in time for us to go to midnight mass on Christmas Eve, and then we can stay up and watch movies and open presents on Christmas morning."

I said what she wouldn't. "And then you're going back to work."

She put her hand on my arm. "You know I'd rather be with you. It'll still feel like Christmas, though. I promise."

But it already didn't. Normally we went the day after Thanksgiving and picked out the perfect Christmas tree. I would inspect every single one until I was sure we selected the very best tree on the lot. Then we'd make a whole day out of decorating it. This year, she had had to work. I was still up, basically sulking, when she got home. She saw how disappointed I was and came up with a "brainstorm." She pulled out an old fake tree she had stashed in the basement from before I was born and decided we should decorate it right then. She was so excited that I didn't want to tell her that just made it worse. Not only did it not feel like Christmastime anymore, but now our house wasn't going to smell like it, either.

"Yeah, okay," I said.

She squeezed my arm. "It will be a great Christmas, you'll see."

I pretended to smile. I didn't want to make her feel guilty. I knew she was still trying to get a handle on her new position at work and how to juggle everything. "I know," I lied.

"That's my girl." She gave me a hug and said good-bye.

I watched as her green scrubs disappeared into the distance. This was going to be the worst Christmas ever. I crumpled up my cup and headed toward the trash. I stopped when I saw who was standing there. Was it possible? It couldn't be—but it was. Old Saint Nick was clearly taking pity on me, because a mere seven feet away, tossing out a half-eaten piece of pizza, was none other than Teo Ortiz.

Seeing him twice in one day?

This had to be fate, and there was no way I was ignoring that.

I mustered up all my courage and walked straight toward him. "I could have told you the pizza was pretty much a hockey puck. Rubbery and yet somehow still as hard as a rock."

"Charlie, right?" he said, his face breaking into a smile. "Where were you ten minutes ago?"

"I wish I could have saved you. But here's a pro tip," I whispered, leaning closer to him. "Go for the sandwiches, yogurts, and cereals. The hot food here is *always* a mess."

"I've been learning that the hard way, so I'll take that under advisement." Could eyes twinkle? Because I was pretty sure his were. "What are you doing here?" he asked.

"My mom's a doctor. I came to say hi. I guess I don't need to ask you the same," I said and gestured toward his large red-and-white-striped shirt. "So I guess this is where you were rushing to earlier. How long have you been volunteering here?"

"Yeah, it's my first day back in a while. I did the candy striper program over the summer, and I figured with the holidays and staff trying to take vacations they could probably use some extra help around now, so I offered to come in a couple of days a week, and they took me up on it."

Okay. Smart, handsome, athletic, conscientious, *and* a volunteer. Forget Ajay. Teo was like Ajay 2.0—the deluxe version.

"What kinds of stuff do you do?" I asked, and to my amazement, I was cool, calm, and collected. Well, I was holding my own, at least.

"Today they have me up on the orthopedic floor, helping escort patients trying to get some movement in," Teo said. "I want to do sports medicine one day, so I like it up there. What kind of doctor is your mom?"

"ER. She loves the pace. She always dreamed about being a doctor. She actually went back to school for it when I was little. I remember when she first started . . ." I let my voice dwindle as he glanced at his phone.

"Sorry," he said. "I—"

"Have to get back to work," I answered for him.

"Yeah, my break ended a minute ago."

"I understand," I told him.

He said good-bye, and I watched him rush off. It seemed like I was doing a lot of that today. But it didn't matter. I got some actual time with Teo, and he wasn't selfish like Morgan feared— in fact, he was the opposite. He was the type of guy I needed.

With everything with my mom, I knew Christmas was going to be a disappointment this year, but with Teo, there was a chance I'd be able to salvage my love life—which meant maybe there was something to look forward to this season, after all.

Four

I picked up the bag of powdered sugar. "Maybe a little extra of this on top," I suggested, studying the jelly doughnuts Morgan had just made.

"Be careful," she warned, "that comes out really fa—"

It was too late; half of the bag dumped out onto the tray, creating what looked like a winter wonderland on Morgan's counter.

"Oh no," I said, trying to shake the excess sugar off the doughnuts. "I'm so sorry."

She laughed. "It's okay, it was just a test batch."

I looked at the mess. "This may be why I handle the business end of our little venture, and you're the talent."

"You think?" she teased.

"I think," I answered, wiping powder off of my nose with the back of my hand. My skills in the kitchen were not exactly world-renowned. I could barely boil pasta or, apparently, coat doughnuts without causing a disaster. But that wasn't going to keep me from trying.

Morgan and I had started a baking business. I spent so much time helping her pick up ingredients and watching her cook her amazing concoctions that I figured we might as well make a profit off it and add *entrepreneur* to our college applications. I was in charge of getting us the gigs, billing, supplies, delivery, and that sort of thing while she came up with the recipes and did the baking. We'd only been doing it about four months, but we'd been getting some decent jobs. Our latest ones included a Hanukkah party for the little kids at Morgan's synagogue, cupcakes for Scobell's Diner, and Christmas cookies for our school's Parent Teacher Association.

She tossed me a wet rag, and I started to clean the counter while she carefully placed the doughnuts into a container. "I think these will work for the Hanukkah party," she said, admiring her fried creations. "The kids should like them. And I'll do some cupcakes with Stars of David on them, and sugar cookies shaped like dreidels."

"Just tell me what and how much of everything you need, and I'll pick it up." We had a pretty good arrangement. I had the car, and she had a monster-sized kitchen that her parents let her take over.

"I think I'll make five dozen *sufganiyot*, six doz—"

"Sufgani-*what*?" I asked.

She laughed. "*Sufganiyot*. It's the Hebrew word for doughnut. It's a traditional Hanukkah food. Like latkes."

"Those I know." Every year during Hanukkah, Morgan's

family had invited me over when they made latkes, fried potato pancakes, which taste pretty incredible. And I had her over to help my mom and me decorate our Christmas tree and overdose on hot chocolate. Or at least most years I did—this one being the exception.

"I'll get you my list for everything tomorrow," she said, and checked the cupcakes cooling on the counter across from me.

They were the ones for Scobell's Diner. I still couldn't believe I had convinced the owner to let us sell them there, but she said she liked my entrepreneurial spirit. And it didn't hurt that she had seen me highlighted on the local news the year before as the winner of the science fair. I did a whole thing on household conservation, efficiency, and lower utility bills. She said my tips saved her money, and she might as well use the savings on supporting young, local businesswomen.

Morgan pulled a bowl of frosting out of the fridge. "Here, stir this to help warm it up a little bit."

"Sooo," I said, keeping my eyes glued to the blue frosting in front of me. "Did we get any more responses to Friday's meeting?"

"You mean since you asked me thirty minutes ago?"

"Well, something new could have come in since then."

She handed me her phone and took the bowl from me. "Check for yourself, but don't be upset if there's no news about Mr. Perfect. Bobby already said Teo hasn't answered him. But it's only been a day."

I was kicking myself for not asking Teo about the meeting myself. I had been caught off guard when I saw him at the hospital and hadn't been thinking a hundred percent clearly.

Although, all things considered, I think I handled myself rather well. Especially since the whole thing was unplanned. "I'm not just checking on *him*. I want to make sure we have enough people so your Secret Santa drawing goes off the way it should."

"Right, I'm sure that's what's concerning you," she teased.

"It is!" Okay, maybe I was slightly concerned about whether Teo would show. I hadn't seen him since I ran into him yesterday, and I wanted that to change.

"I'll pretend to believe you," she said, and put a big glop of frosting into a pastry bag and started icing the cupcakes. "I can't wait for the Secret Santa. I already know the first gift I'm giving my person. I bought a Christmas stocking, and I'm going to make a giant gingerbread man and have him peeking out the top."

Morgan's voice was literally teeming with excitement.

"I do not get why you are so into this," I said.

"Why wouldn't I be?"

"Well, because you're . . ." I let my voice trail off.

"Jewish? So what? I love Christmas. I can still appreciate the holiday even if I don't celebrate it myself. It's about making people happy, being there for them, goodwill to men and all that. Who wouldn't want to take part in that, no matter what they believe?"

"I know. That's not what I meant. It's just, I don't know what's wrong with me. I guess it's Ajay moving on, Noelle's Christmas Ball, the threat of Zakiyah's wrath, no response from Teo, my mom. It's just all adding up. It's making me feel over the holidays already." I was basically going to have to watch everyone around me have the perfect Christmas while I was miserable.

Morgan stopped frosting mid-cupcake. "Okay, you stop that

this second. I'm not letting you be all bah humbug. You just need some Christmas magic. Give me my phone. You can thank me later."

She texted something and then opened the window in her kitchen.

"What are you doing?" I asked. "It's too cold for that."

"Just watch," she said.

A second later, about ten feet away in the house next door, J.D. Ortiz opened a window and stuck his head out. "What's up?"

"Your cousin," she yelled. "He hasn't answered Bobby about the *Sentinel* stuff. We need him. Can you get him to write the article and come to the meeting?"

"What's in it for me?" he asked, giving that cocky smile of his. Of course, instead of just doing something kind for someone, he'd expect something in return.

"I just made doughnuts and cupcakes. You can come take your pick!"

"Be right over," he said.

He shut his window, and I looked at Morgan as if she were out of her mind. "What are you doing? You did not just invite him over here!"

"Yes, I did. And you're going to be nice."

"You said Christmas magic, not a Christmas curse," I muttered. "This is crazy."

"Hey," she reprimanded me. "He's Teo's cousin. They're close. Dealing with J.D. is going to get you what you want. Suck it up. You can do it. Think of it as a science experiment where you have to see how long you can go without sneering at him."

"Might be the first assignment I flunk."

The doorbell rang. "Just remember it's for the greater good," Morgan called out to me as she went to open the door. I braced myself for the worst, which was usually what you could expect when J.D. was involved.

"When I opened my window, I could smell what you were making from my room," J.D. said as he walked into the kitchen.

"That was the plan," she said, opening up the container that held the doughnuts. "Bribe you with my baking—or frying, as the case may be."

He took one and shoved the whole thing in his mouth. He was so disgusting.

Morgan held out the container so he could take another. She laughed as he scarfed it down in less than three seconds. "Okay, you are worse than my brother and Ira."

"I just appreciate good food," he said, popping yet another doughnut in his mouth.

"In that case," I said, "you might want to try chewing."

"She speaks," he responded, his mouth full.

Gross.

Seriously, how did he and Teo share any DNA? I mean, I guess if I was being objective, the two had a slight resemblance. They were both tall, had a similar eye shape and color, a strong jaw-line and dark hair, although Teo wore his short and neat, while J.D. had a mess of curls. And if you looked past J.D.'s personality, they were both attractive. But that was where the similarities ended. Teo was muscular with flawless posture, while J.D. was lanky and slouched all the time. Teo always looked put together, while J.D. looked like he had just crawled out of bed. Teo was an overachiever like me, while J.D. didn't care about anything except for, apparently, taking bribes and eating junk food. There really was no contest.

"So why do you guys want Teo so bad?" he asked.

I was not about to explain myself to him. "It doesn't matter why," I said. "We held up our end; you got your food. What do you care what our reasons are?"

"Whoa!" J.D. held up his hands in defense. "I struck a nerve."

"No, you didn't. It's just none of your business."

"The lady protests too much," he said.

I made a circling motion with my index finger. "Whoop-de-do. He knows a line from *Hamlet*," I said, making sure to keep my voice monotone. "Somebody call the Honor Society pronto."

"You have a crush, don't you?"

"No," I objected.

"Yes, you do. Aww, isn't that cute."

I could feel my face heating up. I had to be cherry red by now. I didn't know what to say, so I just glared at him.

"Don't worry," he said, moving close to me and whispering in my ear. "I won't tell. Well, not today anyway."

I looked to Morgan for help.

"Stop, J.D.," she told him. "Leave her alone. There's no crush. We just think an article by one of the most popular guys in school will help get more eyeballs on the paper. So can you make it happen?"

"For her?" He shook his head. "No. But for you . . . I will do my best."

"Thank you, and . . . ," she said, before showing him out, "invite him to tomorrow's meeting, so we can brief him ahead of time."

Morgan was a genius. Now I would get even more time with Teo. I owed her one.

"Fine," J.D. answered. "But I do think that calls for a few more doughnuts."

Morgan went and got the rest of the batch and handed the whole thing to him. "Just bring back the container when you're done."

"Absolutely." He bowed. "Pleasure doing business with you."

She closed the door behind him.

"I cannot stand him," I growled once he was gone. "I swear every day he gets worse."

"Well, you weren't exactly warm and fuzzy yourself."

"Because he's awful." I picked up the pastry bag and finished icing the half-frosted cupcake. "If I lived next to him, I'd make my mom move."

"He's not that bad," she said. "Remember when my dad broke his leg last year? J.D. shoveled our sidewalk. He wouldn't even take any money. He can be really nice. He taught my brother how to skateboard, he showed me how to use Photoshop, and he gave me his English notes when I was out sick last month."

I hadn't even realized my hands had tightened into fists until I saw the giant blob of frosting that was now half on the cupcake, half on the counter.

"*Nice?* Whose side are you on?" I asked, cleaning up my mess.

"Yours, of course," she answered. "I just think that maybe you should give him a chance."

I had given him chances. Every week since the beginning of the school year. And every week he gave me problems. A fight over assignments, deadlines, picture selection, anything to give me a hard time. Something Morgan seemed to forget. "How about if we see if he comes through with Teo first?"

"Okay, but he will," she said. "You'll see. Have a little faith."

Too bad having faith in J.D. was a lot easier said than done.

Five

"How long do you think you'll be?" Ira asked Morgan when we got to the computer lab for our meeting.

"Not too long," she answered. "It's just a quick update with the editors to make sure they're all set for Friday."

"I'll wait for you then," he said.

"You sure?" She was looking up at him adoringly. "You don't have to."

He was mirroring her doe-eyed, smitten look. "I want to."

Of course he did. It was getting harder and harder to spend time with Morgan without Ira around. It's not that I didn't like him, or that they treated me like a third wheel—they didn't. But it was still hard not to feel like I was intruding. Or maybe I was just more aware of their coupledom now that I was solo. You'd think after all these years, Ira and Morgan would want to spend less time together. But it was the opposite. They couldn't get enough of each other.

Ira wrapped his arms around her and pulled her closer, as Morgan leaned in and gave him a small peck on the lips.

I swear they were so disgustingly cute. It had always been that way. Even from the beginning. When Morgan's family moved to town five years ago, it was right around the Jewish New Year. Ira's family invited them over to celebrate. The two hit it off instantly and began talking and flirting every day. They went to the dance together and have been a couple ever since.

"You guys are going to make me sick," I told them.

"That's our goal," Morgan said.

"Well, I'm going inside." People were already making their way into the computer lab. "Don't be late."

"I wouldn't dream of it," she said, pretending to be all serious. "There's no way I'd waste one of my valuable passes."

"I don't blame you," I said, laughing. "People would kill for those." For part of Morgan's birthday present two years ago, I had given her some "late passes." I may have a slight tendency to overreact when people don't show up on time (especially if they don't text or it's not for a good reason). So to keep the peace, I gave Morgan five passes that she can use when she's late—no explanations or apologies necessary—and I can't complain or hold a grudge. As of now, she's only used two.

I looked up at the clock. Everyone still had five minutes to get there. So far, we were missing about half—including Teo.

What if J.D. hadn't come through? He was going to owe

Morgan a million doughnuts. I didn't have to worry long, though, because thirty seconds later, Teo strode into the room.

He gave a wave in my direction, and I took that as an invitation to go say hello. "I'm happy you were able to come," I said. I had planned this conversation down to the last detail. Pleasant greeting, check. Now if all went according to plan, he'd give one in return, I'd bring up his past *Sentinel* work, he'd ask about mine, I'd say how much I love working on the holiday edition—that I love the holidays and all the amazing celebrations this time of year, and then I'd plant the first seed about Noelle's Christmas Ball.

"Yeah, I'm glad J.D. told me about it. My schedule had been a little crazy, but with football winding down, I can pick up a story or two." Return pleasantry—success.

"You did a bunch of stuff for the *Sentinel* before, didn't you?" I asked, everything going like clockwork.

"Last year I—"

"Teo," Bobby said, slapping him on the shoulder. "You made it."

I gave him a death glare to leave, but Bobby either didn't notice it or didn't care.

"Yeah, man, sorry I didn't get back to you sooner," Teo said. "Your message went into my junk mail. I didn't see it until J.D. told me about it, and I went looking."

As if it wasn't annoying enough that Bobby hijacked my conversation, it went from bad to worse. Katie Boon came in, and she started gushing about Teo being there, too. Pretty soon, Teo was swarmed by just about every editor. They were all trying to chat him up and get his attention. Not that I could really blame them. Who wouldn't want to spend time with him?

By the time I called the meeting to order, I was feeling a little defeated. Friday, the full staff was going to be here. If I couldn't get any Teo time with this small group, trying to have it with everyone around was just going to be worse. The newspaper meetings were supposed to be my time to get to know Teo better. I was going to need a new plan.

Despite everything falling apart, Morgan and I kept our word. The meeting was super short. Short enough that J.D. missed the whole thing. He strolled in right as everyone was getting up to go. He didn't even apologize.

I wanted to say something, but I bit my tongue. I wasn't going to start up with his cousin right there.

"We'll see you all Friday," Morgan called out. "And don't forget we'll have the Secret Santa drawing."

She was way too chipper.

"Cool," Teo said. "See you guys then." He looked right at me, bowed his head, and gave me a little salute. It was pretty adorable. I wanted to rush after him and finish our earlier conversation, but J.D. was by his side and ushering him out.

Why did J.D. have to come at all? If he was going to be that late, he should have just stayed away. "J.D. ruins everything again," I mumbled when it was just me and Morgan.

"He did get Teo here," she reminded me.

"True." But it didn't improve my chances of him going with me to Noelle's party.

Ira stuck his head in the door. "Okay to come in?"

"Yeah," I said.

"Did all your dreams come true?" he asked me, hopping on a desk next to Morgan.

"Hardly," I said. I had let Morgan fill him in on my situation. "I don't know how I'm going to move this forward. Teo and I have no classes together, I never see him in the halls, and the hospital run-in was a fluke. These meetings were supposed to be my in."

"Just ask him out," Ira said.

Like that was so easy. I had no idea if Teo was remotely interested in me that way. There was no way I was going to risk that rejection. I wanted to let him get to know me first. "Not happening."

"Maybe you can be extra flirty during the paper's holiday party," Morgan said. "I can bring in some mistletoe."

That was a hard no. "Not only would that be ridiculously embarrassing, it'd also be too late. The timing of the party is too close to Noelle's."

"Too bad you couldn't get his name in the Secret Santa," she said.

"Right?" I joked. "Then I could give him five perfect gifts to pique his curiosity and show him how compatible we truly are."

Morgan clutched her hands over her heart, whipped her dirty-blond hair to one side, and put on her most overdramatic voice. "Then just like in a cheesy movie, when the big reveal happens, you'll lock eyes and know you're meant to be a couple—or at the very least go to the Christmas Ball together."

"Yeah," I said, my head spinning with possibilities. "It could totally win over his heart."

"Wait," Morgan said, her voice returning to normal. "You know I'm kidding, right?"

I did. I mean, I had been, too—until I realized it could actually work. "Guys, I think this is it. This is how I'm going to win him over."

They both looked more than a little skeptical, but what did they know? I was the one who loved science. The one who liked to analyze data and draw hypotheses, and I was sure that I could prove this one right.

"You don't get to choose your Secret Santa," Ira reminded me.

That's what he thought.

I was already formulating a plan.

Six

I met up with Morgan right before homeroom. I was not the type of person who skipped down halls, but if I were—this would have been my moment to do it. Operation Secret Santa (as I was now calling it) was just hours from taking off. And I felt like pirouetting, cartwheeling, and leaping as I walked. Everything was set to go.

"Today's the day!" I clapped my hands together. "My plan to win over Teo Ortiz officially goes into motion."

Morgan fiddled with the hem of her sweater. "Are you sure you want to go through with this?"

"Of course I'm sure. It's practically all I've been able to think about." I studied her face. "What? Why are you looking at me like that?"

"Like what?" Morgan asked, averting her eyes to the ground.

"Like I'm going to mess this up!"

"I never said that."

"You didn't have to!" That was the thing with a best friend—you knew what was going on in their head, even when you wished you didn't. "This is going to work, I know it."

She gave me that look again.

"What?" I cried.

"It's just that you don't know how to break a rule. *Any* rule. Are you sure you can do this?"

"I'm not trying to hack into the computer system and change my grades—which, FYI, I'm sure I could do if I really wanted—I'm RIGGING A SECRET SANTA drawing." I slapped my hand over my mouth and glanced around the hall to make sure no one else heard me. I was in the clear. "It's not a big deal."

"Says the girl who broke down after taking an extra piece of candy from Mrs. Chevian's doorstep on Halloween."

"I was eight!" I regretted ever telling her that story. When I was trick-or-treating in third grade, the Chevians left a bowl of candy on their stoop with a sign that said TAKE ONE. I took two, but I felt so guilty that by the end of the night I was in tears and went back the next day to apologize.

"Okay, then what about last year, the last day of school?" she asked.

I shrugged. "What about it?"

"Charlie!"

"Fine, yes, everyone who had final-period study hall was skipping it to go get pizza. Except for me. I couldn't do it. But this is different. The candy, the cutting class, that was doing something wrong. This isn't. This is for love. And besides," I said, giving her what I hoped was an endearing smile, "you weren't there for either of those things. If you had lived in town when I was in third grade or were in my study hall last year, I would have been fine. But you're here now. Nothing bad is going to happen. I'm sure of it."

She shook her head. "Okay, I'm in." She sighed. "You know that. Let's get you the boy of your dreams."

"Thank you, thank you, thank you," I said and hugged my arms around my chest. This was so going to work.

Seven

I adjusted the chairs in the computer lab so they were in a perfectly spaced circle, put my coat on the back of the one with a
direct line of sight to the door, and pushed a small desk in front
of my seat. I had gotten to the meeting extra early to ensure I'd
be the first one there. It was important that I be in control of all
aspects of the Secret Santa drawing in order for it to go smoothly.

I was sure I'd thought of everything down to the last detail—
including the mason jar I brought from home. I carefully took it
out of my bag and placed it on the desk along with the tiny slips
of paper I cut up last night.

Katie and Zakiyah came into the room a few minutes later.

"My Secret Santa better get me something good," Zakiyah
said as she reached for a little slip of paper.

I pushed them away from her. "I'll fill them all out," I said.

"Wouldn't it be easier if we all did our own?" she asked.

Of course it would, but then I wouldn't have been able to keep Teo's name from going in the jar. And right now, a slip of paper with his name on it was safely tucked away in my pocket.

"I want to make sure all of the names are legible," I explained. "That way there won't be any confusion."

Zakiyah sneered at me. "I think I can fill out my own name."

She reached for the slip again, and I grabbed them all away. "I want them to be consistent," I growled.

Zakiyah curled her lip at me. "What is wrong with you?"

"Nothing."

"Just let it go," Katie whispered to her. "You know how she is."

"Yeah, insane," she said as they went to take seats. "Always has to get her way. How does she even know everyone wants to take part?"

"I'll ask them," I answered.

"Wasn't talking to you," Zakiyah said.

Whatever, let her be mad. It wasn't like Zakiyah and I hadn't had our issues before. Besides, this wasn't about her. It was about Teo and me.

I held my breath every time someone entered the room. And right on time, Teo walked in. I loved his punctuality. I didn't even bother to hide my grin. He smiled back, and I knew I was doing the right thing with this whole Secret Santa plan.

Morgan made me wait a few minutes for the stragglers before we got started, even though J.D. was the only one who walked in late.

As talk about themes, deadlines, and word counts dwindled

42

down, I checked that everyone wanted to be a part of the Secret Santa.

"When is the party again?" Teo asked.

"The Friday before vacation," I told him, giving him my most flirty smile.

"Really?" Zakiyah said, interrupting my moment. "We finally get out of school, and you want us to stay in the building even longer? Why don't we do the week before?"

"This was discussed already," I reminded her. "At a meeting *you* were at, even though you weren't supposed to be."

"Sue me for not hanging on your every word," she said. "But my point still stands."

She was not messing this up for me. "We need enough time for the Secret Santa," I informed her, nipping the suggestion in the bud. Things couldn't change. I already had everything mapped out, like the days I'd give Teo his gifts, my "accidental" run-ins, and so on. I wasn't about to go back to the drawing board.

Zakiyah was shooting daggers at me, so Morgan jumped in. "It's a celebration of the holiday *and* the paper coming out. Some of us will be on crazy deadlines before then, so that's really the only day that we can do it. Sure, we'll still be in school. But it's not for work. It's for fun. And it will only be an hour or so. Some food, drinks, presents, friends. Come on, we deserve this! What do you say?"

They all nodded. Morgan was definitely better with people than I was. I put everyone's name in the jar as she made a list of what everyone was going to bring to the party.

When I finished, Zakiyah came up and grabbed the jar.

"Uh . . . what are you doing?" I asked.

"Getting this meeting over with." She handed the jar to Katie, who was to my left, and told her to take one and pass it around.

I jumped up. "I'll make sure everyone takes one."

"We've got it," Zakiyah said. "You'll get your turn. It will make its way back to you." She rolled her eyes as she returned to her seat—right next to Teo. Of course, she put herself next to the hottest guy in the room. Not that that mattered now. I had bigger problems.

I didn't know what to do. I was supposed to draw first, so I could pretend to pull out my premade slip, but the jar was already making the rounds. I had to stop this. Only how? I couldn't make a scene, not with Teo there. But if I didn't, by the time the jar got to me, they'd realize we were one name short.

If I didn't know better, I would have thought this was Zakiyah's revenge for gutting most of her gossip column. I was fine with the who's dating who, and who got into their dream colleges—but the breakups and rejections just seemed mean. Only next edition, she'd have a real scoop: COEDITOR OF THE PAPER RIGS SECRET SANTA DRAWING. And I wouldn't even be able to edit it out. That would just be asking for her to spread it over every social media channel imaginable. I was done for.

The jar made it halfway around the room. Zakiyah had just reached in, and I still didn't have a plan. "Seriously," she said, studying her slip. "Does someone want to trade?"

She probably got my name. Although three of her exes worked on the paper, so it really could have been any of us. But honestly, it didn't matter. That was the least of my concerns.

44

There had to be a way to fix this. I was smart. I could come up with something. I wasn't trying to cover up some diabolical plot, just a silly holiday game. This was a no-brainer. *Think, Charlie!* Okay, I could just get up, walk over to the jar, pretend to trip, and knock it over. *Who am I kidding? That won't work.* Everyone would know I did it on purpose. It was way too obvious. Maybe I could pretend one of the slips of paper fell under my desk and that I just found it. Only then I'd have to throw Teo's name in the jar and ruin my chances of getting it. I could wait until the jar came around to me and then magically find the slip of paper on the floor, but what if someone called for a do-over? Zakiyah was bound to ask for one. She had made it clear she wasn't happy with her pick.

I didn't have any choice. I was going to have to risk it. Either that or admit that I tampered with the drawing—which wasn't an option.

Only I waited too long.

The jar made it to Ruthie Gruber, who was sitting to my right. "Hey," she said, reaching her hand into the jar. "There's not enough. This is the last one. Someone's name was left out."

"I told you we should have all put our own names in," Zakiyah called out.

Why hadn't I moved faster? How was I going to get Teo's slip on the floor without everyone noticing?! I reached my hand into my pockets, but they were sweaty and shaking. "Um, I . . . um, I, uh, filled out everyone's names. Maybe one of them, um, fell." I got down on my knees and pretended to look around. So much for appearing calm and cool and in my element. I just wanted to disappear. How bad would crawling to the other side of the room and curling up into a ball in the corner until everyone left look? This was what I got for trying to break the rules once in my life. Morgan was right; I was an awful liar. Why had I even tried?

"Let's just fill out new slips and start over," Zakiyah said. "I want to get out of here."

I got up and nodded. It was over. I had lost.

Morgan was staring at me with an I-told-you-so look mixed with pity. I closed my eyes and willed away the tears that were threatening to show themselves. Why had I been so stupid?

Zakiyah pulled out some paper and started tearing it into little slips.

"Wait!" Morgan called out over everyone's chatter. "Don't kill me. We don't have to do it over. We're good. It's totally my fault. I accidentally took two names. The papers were stuck together. I'm sorry. I'll give the extra to Charlie. I'll see most of you next week. Everyone else, I'll see you at the party."

Wait, what?!!

Was I hearing correctly? Had my best friend really come through again?

I sat there frozen as everyone but Morgan filed out of the room. I still couldn't believe this worked.

"Merry Christmas," she said and smiled. "You got what you wanted. Do I give the best gifts or what?"

"You do," I said, my whole body finally relaxing. I . . . well, Morgan . . . actually pulled off my plan.

"I know," she said and did a little victory dance. "I told you I had your back."

"Thank you," I said. But it wasn't just for the Secret Santa help. It was for everything. Morgan was always there for me, no matter what. My boy situation was still a work in progress, but I definitely got an A when it came to picking a best friend. And with her help, I knew I could make the Teo operation a success.

I was going to have a date to the Christmas Ball. I could feel it.

Eight

S core," I called out as I pulled into one of the best parking spots at Sandbrook Mall. "Your superpower has come through again," I told Morgan and drummed on the steering wheel in excitement. The shopping trip for Teo was already off to a great start.

Morgan laughed. "Glad to be of service."

The girl had the absolute best luck in the world when it came to finding spots. It was like the parking gods watched over her, even during the holiday rush, and got her a spot in seconds. There were dozens of cars still circling, but not us!

"And before we go in," she said, pulling a small container from her bag, "some sustenance."

My mouth was already beginning to salivate. "Oh my gosh! Have I told you how much I love you?"

"Yeah, I'm the best," she said jokingly. Only it was no joke. Morgan took off the lid and the smell of cinnamon-sugary yum-miness filled the car. It was her famous snickerdoodles. After I stuffed what had to be the eighth one in my mouth, we were ready to hit the mall. "Those are incredible," I told her. "The PTA is going to be demanding more after they get a taste of these." They really were addictive. All of Morgan's creations were. I had gained fifteen pounds since she and I started our bakery busi-ness, and at this rate I'd put on a few more by Christmas. There was a good chance I'd have to start wearing stretchy pants to school, but I didn't care. It was worth it. "The only problem is, I may be eating all of our profits."

"Hey," she said, slightly knocking her shoulder against mine, "if it gets you back in the holiday spirit, it's all good."

"Thanks." The truth was, I was finally starting to feel like my old self. I may not have been getting my usual Christmas, but Operation Secret Santa gave me something to look forward to. It would let me spread Christmas cheer *and* snag the perfect guy to kiss under the mistletoe at Noelle's party.

I felt a rush when we walked inside. Some things never changed; you could always count on the mall to remind you it was holiday time. The throngs of people headed in every direc-tion, the holiday decorations as far as the eye could see, the scent—I was fairly certain they pumped a pine fragrance into the air—and, of course, the sounds: the chatter of kids and parents finishing their shopping lists and the Christmas music that filled the space. Holiday songs always made me smile, but the fact that

"All I Want for Christmas Is You" was playing made it even better. It felt like another sign that I was headed in the right direction.

"Where to first?" Morgan asked.

I pulled out my list. Last night, I went over a map of the mall and planned out the most efficient course of action. "We start out on the lower level with the sporting goods store, and then make a beeline down winter village." Every Christmas the mall set out a row of little kiosks that sold all sorts of gifts—everything from snow globes, candles, and ornaments to jewelry, wallets, specialty foods, and more. "Then we head to the upper level and stop at the bookstore, Funny or What gifts, and finish at Jordan's." I saved the best for last. Jordan's was one of the most popular stores in the mall. Partially because it had these awesome massage chairs that you could sit in and the employees rarely kicked you out, but also because it had really cool stuff. All the latest electronics, app-controlled devices, gadgets like glasses and pens that had recorders in them, games, consoles, and more. I figured after all that shopping, we could reward ourselves with a well-deserved massage.

The sporting goods store wound up being a bust. Nothing called out *Teo.*

"Want to try the sports boutique?" Morgan asked.

I shook my head. I specifically left that off my list. "I don't know which players are his favorite." Not for lack of trying. I had studied his GroupIt page in depth to prepare for today. I looked over every single picture, every post, every interest. I was going to know the perfect gifts when I saw them. "It's okay. We have a

50

lot of places to look at." I wasn't deterred; I hadn't really expected to find anything at the first store.

But my confidence was starting to wane when I came up empty at winter village, the bookstore, and Funny or What. Turned out that looking at someone's selfies and photos of their ski trip, birthday, and other random events didn't make you an expert on them. I couldn't even pick out one book I thought suited Teo, let alone five of them.

I let out a huge sigh. "Well, this isn't going like I planned. Did you see anything?" I asked Morgan.

"No, this is hard."

"Impossible," I corrected her.

"Hey, we are not giving up," Morgan said, her voice sounding optimistic. "There's still Jordan's."

She was right. I wasn't done yet. I could do this. I wasn't a quitter. "Yeah, totally, it has everything." I'd find something there.

And I did. Lots of amazing somethings. For *me*. As for *Teo*? I was at a loss. Not only did nothing call out his name, but everything was so expensive. I wanted to get him something nice, but I didn't have a gazillion dollars to spend.

A knot was forming in my neck. A massage in one of the store's chairs would have helped, but two kids were camped out in them and showed no sign of moving.

Nothing was going right. Just when I thought maybe the holidays were looking up, my plans fell apart. I couldn't show Teo how well I knew him, because I didn't. So much for five perfect gifts. I couldn't even come up with one semi-okay one. I walked out of the store and leaned against the wall.

"This sucks," I muttered. Not even "Winter Wonderland," one of my favorite Christmas songs of all time, blasting through the speakers was going to improve my mood. "Any ideas?" I asked Morgan, hoping she had a burst of inspiration.

"Still no clue. I had a hard enough time thinking of something for Ira, and he gave me hints. I barely know Teo. I wouldn't even know where to start."

That was the problem.

Neither did I.

But I knew someone who would. Now, the question was, could I bring myself to ask him?

Nine

Don't do it, Charlie. Don't do it. Leave now. It's not too late. I turned around and headed away from J.D. Ortiz's house, but I only made it about three feet before I made a one-eighty and was back at his doorstep. *Do not push that doorbell. Don't do it. You will regret it. You can come up with your own ideas. You don't need J.D.'s help. You are better than this.* Only I wasn't. If I wanted to get Teo personalized gifts, I needed someone who knew him personally. But did it have to be J.D.?

I turned to leave again. Then back around. I may have repeated that move three or four times. I didn't know what to do. But I couldn't stand there forever. I had to make up my mind. *I can do this. I can do this. No, I can't.*

This was a stupid idea. I was going home. I should have just dropped Morgan off and kept driving in the first place. I'd just buy Teo a Starbucks card and some chocolate snowmen and be done with it. Operation Secret Santa was officially over.

I'd made it down the steps when I heard the door open.

"So," J.D. said, with one eyebrow raised, "did you just come to spin around at my doorway or did you want something?"

Crap. Why did he have to see me? "Don't worry about it. Forget I was here."

"Yeah . . ." He hemmed. "I don't know that I'll be able to unsee that." Then he mimicked my awkward turns back and forth. "If it's dance lessons you're after, I agree, you need them. But I'm probably not the guy."

"Good to know," I said and continued down his walkway.

"Wait," he called after me. "Are you really not going to tell me why you're here?"

I have already made a fool of myself; should I just ask for his help? It's not like it can get any worse. Only I knew that wasn't true. Still . . . I was already there . . . "Fine," I said. "I have an offering. These"—I held up the half-eaten container of Morgan's snickerdoodles—"in exchange for your help."

"Help with what?"

"You have to swear this stays between us," I said, and walked back over to him.

"How can I swear when I don't know what I'm swearing to?"

"You are just swearing to keep a secret."

"But if I don't know the secret . . ."

I turned around again. "I knew this was a bad idea. Forget it."

"Okay, okay," he said. "I swear."

I held out my pinkie finger.

54

"You've got to be kidding."

"Just do it," I instructed.

"Solely for the sake of curiosity," he said as he did the pinkie promise with me. "Now do you want to come in and tell me your big confession, or would you rather stay out here? It's pretty cold out."

"Fine." I followed him inside, and he offered me a seat in the living room. I don't know what I was expecting his house to look like, but not this. It had a warm, homey feeling. Almost rustic. I guess I expected something a little more scattered, kind of like J.D.

I perched myself on the edge of a leather recliner and looked around the room. There was a large fireplace with pictures of J.D. and what I'm guessing were his parents and older sister lining the top. In the corner of the room were two boxes that said *Christmas decorations*, but they hadn't been unpacked, and there was no tree in sight.

J.D. must have seen where I was looking. "We get our tree about a week or two before the holiday, so it doesn't lose its needles," he said.

"Wait. You get a Douglas?! Why? A Fraser fir will last a lot longer, and you can put it up so much earlier."

He gave me that smirk of his again. "Is this what you came to talk about? My family's choice of tree?"

"No, sorry." I had very strong opinions when it came to Christmas trees. But I really wasn't one to talk. Not this year.

"So are you going to tell me this secret of yours? What do you want from me?"

"Your help," I said. "I picked Teo's name for the Secret Santa, and I want to get him things he'll really like. And I don't know where to start."

J.D. was sitting kitty-corner to me, on a comfy-looking, copper-colored couch. "I was right," he said, shaking his head. "You do have a crush on him."

"I do not. I just want to be a good Secret Santa."

He wasn't buying it.

He sat back on the couch in one of those power poses with his hands behind his head. "Sure," he said. "That's why you're willing to come talk to someone you can't stand, because you want to be a nice gift giver?"

"Fine. Whatever. Maybe I have a small crush. And I never said I can't stand—" I stopped myself. We both knew that wasn't true. J.D. and I couldn't even talk newspaper stuff without Morgan in the room as a go-between. "We just have different visions for the paper. It's not personal."

"You sure about that?" he asked.

I ignored his question. "Are you going to help me or not?"

"What's in it for me again?"

"I told you," I said, holding out the cookies. "These."

He shook his head. "You're going to have to do a lot better than that."

"Fine, every batch of baked goods we make for our company for the next month, we'll save you some. Sound good?"

"Not even close."

"Two months?"

He shook his head again.

He was so annoying. "What do you want, then?"

J.D. leaned in closer to me. "I want full editorial control of all the photos that go into the holiday edition of the paper. And that includes a full-page photo spread."

"No way."

He leaned back into the couch. "Then I guess Teo is going to get some pretty bad presents from his Secret Santa. I bet he'll be really disappointed. You know, I think he dumped his last girlfriend because she gave him a crappy birthday gift."

"Ha-ha," I said. I knew he was lying. I knew he was just trying to egg me on. But I also knew he had me in a tight spot. He was the key to what I really wanted. "How about," I offered, "we include the photo spread, but I have final say on what goes in it?"

"Pass," he said.

"I can't give you full control."

"Actually, you can. What do you think I'm going to put in there?"

"Oh, I don't know," I said, and before I realized it, I was standing up. "Maybe cheerleading tryout photos that show no cheerleaders."

"I told you, the one with just the pom-poms in the air was a better photo. The composition, the lighting—"

"People like seeing themselves in the paper. They pick it up hoping they'll be in it."

"They have GroupIt and every other social media platform in the world for that," he said, jumping up. "My photo represented all of the people who tried out, not just a select few."

"But I told you what I wanted. It wasn't your call to make."

"And that's why," he said, "I want full control. I'm a good photographer. I'm good with layout. I deserve this. It's not asking a lot."

It was to someone who liked having things done a very particular way. But *maybe* it didn't *have* to be my vision all the time. I sat back down.

"I won't put anything 'distasteful' in," he said, making air quotes, "if that's what you're worried about." It wasn't. "I'll even listen to reasonable questions and requests," J.D. added. "But I will have the final say. Okay?"

"If I agree to this, and I'm not saying that I am," I countered, "then I want more than just gift guidance. I want quality time with Teo. You'll have to help me get to know him and spend time with him."

"I can make that happen." He smiled, the dimple in his left cheek on full display. "Deal?"

He put out his hand, and I shook it. "Deal."

What had I just gotten myself into?

Ten

We should go to the mall tomorrow and pick out the first gift, I texted J.D. later that night.

K, he wrote back.

What time? I asked.

I don't know. We'll figure it out tomorrow.

Seriously, tomorrow?! *I need a time,* I typed back. *So I can plan accordingly.*

I could almost feel him rolling his eyes at me through the phone, but I wasn't trying to be difficult. I just wasn't one for playing things by ear. Not having a locked-in schedule made me feel antsy. Like my brain had an itch that, of course, was impossible to scratch.

Fine, btwn 12 & 3:30, he answered.

I squeezed the phone in my hand. He was seriously testing

my last nerve. But I had to stay calm. *Can you please be a little more specific?*

Three little dots popped up on my phone, which meant he was typing. They disappeared but there was no message. It happened again. He was probably debating which snarky response he wanted to send.

Instead he just wrote, *Have something in the morning. Not sure when I'll be done.*

I wanted to remind him that he owed me. That if he wanted to have control of the *Sentinel*'s photos, he needed to help me. But I knew I had no right to dictate his schedule, even if it meant me having to work around his. Still, I didn't want to sit around all day waiting for him to call. I'd go stir crazy and get nothing done. *How about we just plan for 3:30?* I wrote.

Fine, whatever, he replied.

It wasn't an ideal response, but it would do. I told him I'd pick him up, and the next day at 3:30 p.m. sharp, I pulled into his driveway and honked the horn.

Ten whole minutes later, he got in the car.

"We said 3:30," I reminded him.

"I was backing up a project. It took longer than I thought. I didn't want to risk losing it."

I tutted my tongue at him.

"What? I texted you at one and said I could go to the mall earlier if you wanted. You were the one who said no, so I started work on something else." His eyebrows furrowed together. "Stop looking at me like that. It wasn't like I made you sit out here in the car. I invited you inside. You were the one who refused."

I thought it would make him move faster if he knew I was waiting outside. Clearly, I was wrong. I put the car into reverse and backed out of the driveway without responding.

"So you're not going to speak to me for the rest of the day, is that it? This trip is gonna be fun."

He had a point. And I *was* going to have to talk to him if I wanted to get his advice about Teo's gifts. "Okay," I said. "I'll let it go. It's just lateness is a huge pet peeve of mine. I'm always on time, and when someone else isn't and keeps me waiting, it's like they're saying their time is more important than mine. It's rude."

We were both silent for a moment. "I'm sorry," he said, his voice softer than before. "I'll try to be better."

I nodded. "What were you working on?" I asked, trying to change the subject to something more neutral.

"I've been interning at this 3-D printing company, Making Your Mark. It's really cool. You can use one of their designs or submit your own and they print it up. It can be anything. A toy, silverware, jewelry." He held up his phone. "I made this case." The whole thing was plastic, but there were tiny curved lines cut out of it that added texture. I had never seen anything like it.

"That's pretty cool."

"It's my fingerprint. Well," he said, his speech getting faster. "A blown-up version of it anyway. It was a photo I took that I was able to program into the printer."

"The company just let you do that?"

"Yeah, the people who work there are really awesome. And I guess they figure since they're not paying me, the least they can do is teach me something and let me play around. When you showed up, I was backing up a new design I've been working on. I'm trying to make my mom's Christmas gift on the printer. I'm almost ready for the test prototype stage."

I had never seen him so excited about something. Not that we really had that many civil conversations. "Wow, impressive. I'm sure your mom will love it."

He shrugged. "I hope so. I like to think I'm a pretty good gift giver."

"Well, I'm pretty much counting on that," I said as we turned into the mall parking lot. Now was his chance to prove himself. I seriously hoped he didn't disappoint.

Eleven

Well, if Morgan had stellar parking karma, J.D. had the opposite.

He pointed to his right. "There's a spot over there."

"And two cars waiting for it."

"What about on the other side of the lot?" he suggested.

"We just came from there." I squeezed on the steering wheel to keep from shouting. We'd been going in circles for twenty minutes. The actual shopping hadn't even started, and I was already frustrated.

"Something will open eventually." He was annoyingly relaxed.

I couldn't take it anymore. I wasn't going to wait for fate, I was going to create it. I pulled up to the front of the mall and rolled down my window. A man and his child had just exited. "Excuse me, sir," I called out. "I'm hoping to grab your spot. Can you give me a heads-up which way?"

He told me, and a couple of minutes later, J.D. and I were finally parked. "See, that's how you get things done," I informed him.

"Says the girl who drove around for an hour before coming up with that brainstorm."

"It wasn't an hour, and I didn't see you coming up with any bright ideas." I power walked to the door, and J.D. matched my pace.

He smiled when we walked inside, but the magic of the mall and all its Christmastime glory was wasted on me. Yesterday, the twinkly lights, the winter village, the poinsettias, the miles of garland, and blasts of holiday music invigorated me; today they felt like a cruel reminder that you don't always get what you want for Christmas. A point punctuated by the fact that I was intentionally in the mall with J.D. Ortiz.

"Let's start with that little sports boutique," I said. I skipped Fanmania yesterday, but now with J.D. there, it was probably my best shot to find something. Sports fanatics loved the place. It had memorabilia, autographed photos, rare cards, and more.

The mall was packed, same as yesterday, but I seemed more attuned to it today. I was sick of all the texters and people with their heads in the clouds thinking I'd move so they could walk haphazardly around without paying attention. I wasn't having it. Yes, that meant no fewer than four people managed to bump into me as we headed to Fanmania, but so what? Maybe it would teach them a lesson. I know Morgan would have bah humbugged my attitude again. But she wasn't here. J.D. was—which only added to my mood.

The walls of Fanmania were covered with cards and autographed pictures. We'd definitely get one, maybe even a few gifts here. Then I could get home. I clapped my hands together. "Okay, who's Teo's favorite player?"

"Which sport?"

"I don't know. I guess football; that's what he plays."

"He plays baseball, too, when it's the season," J.D. said, picking up a baseball from the counter, tossing it in the air, and catching it.

"Oh, right," I said. "Either's fine."

"He's a huge fan of Manny Franco."

"Yeah, Manny. That sounds good," I said.

"You have no idea who that is, do you?"

I didn't want to confess that I didn't. I hated not knowing things. Even more so, I hated admitting it. But J.D. didn't make me say it. He just smiled. "It's okay," he whispered. "I wouldn't either if it wasn't for Teo and my uncle. Sports aren't really my thing."

I wasn't sure why he was being so nice.

"Manny's a retired baseball player. Played for a few teams during his career. Has three championship rings. Splits his time between Miami and Stamford now."

"Can I help you?" the woman behind the counter asked, interrupting J.D.'s mini baseball lesson.

65

"Anything of Manny Franco's?" I asked.

"A signed baseball, picture, and card. Take your pick," she said.

They all sounded like decent options. "How about the baseball?"

She tapped the top of the display case in front of her. "It's thirteen hundred dollars."

"Thirteen hundred?!" I choked on the words, and J.D. carefully placed the baseball he was tossing back on the counter.

The lady winked at J.D. "Don't worry, that one's just a regular four-dollar baseball."

I think I heard him breathe a sigh of relief.

"Um," I said, "do you maybe have something of Manny's that's cheaper? Like maybe the baseball card?"

"That'll still run you several hundred."

"Okay, thank you," I said. "I'll think about it." Yeah, I was going to think about how never in a million years did I think a baseball card would cost so much money. It was a piece of paper with someone's picture and a signature. I thought it'd be twenty bucks tops.

"Well, this is about as successful as yesterday," I said when we left the store. "I was hoping to spend twenty-five dollars, fifty max—and that was on all the gifts."

"Come on," he said, and started walking away from me. "Let's go to Jordan's."

"I've already been through the whole store. I can't afford it. There's nothing there."

"There's something," he said.

Well, he did know Teo better than I did. Maybe there was something I missed. I quickened my stride to catch up to him.

Once inside the store, J.D. walked like a man with a purpose. He really did have something in mind! For a split second, I let myself get excited. Until I saw where he stopped.

J.D. plopped himself in one of the massage chairs.

"THIS is why you wanted to come here?" I whisper-screamed, so my volume wouldn't cause a scene. "You are supposed to be helping me shop, not sitting down on the job."

"What? It's just a quick break. And look how lucky—this chair was empty."

I didn't even have the words. I just spun around on my heels and stormed out.

He was unbelievable. I was so angry. I leaned against the railing, looking out onto the lower floor. Why couldn't it be January already? I was so ready for this season to be over. Nothing was the way it should be. I even had to open my Advent calendar on my own. It wasn't like it was a huge thing, but Mom and I had always done it together in the past. I picked at a bright-red bow tied around some garland and took a deep breath. Everything around me looked like Christmas, but it didn't feel like it. Or maybe like the Grinch, my heart had become two sizes too small. Only there was nothing around to help it grow.

"Hey," J.D. said, walking over to me. "Why are you getting so worked up?"

I yanked at the bow. "Maybe because this whole thing was a waste of time. I should never have asked you for help to begin with. I'm not going to find anything for Teo, and I'm just going to have to deal with it."

"You give up way too easily," he said.

Was he serious? I turned to face him. "It's not giving up. It's being realistic. I don't need to spend another three hours in the mall to know it's hopeless."

"Well, I could have told you this place was a waste of time."

"Excuse me?!"

"I mean, you don't go to the mall if you don't want to spend money. What did you really think you'd find for five bucks a gift?"

"I don't know." I fought to keep my voice at a normal decibel. "If you knew we wouldn't find anything, why didn't you tell me?"

"Because you wanted to come. And have you ever tried telling someone like you something they don't want to hear? I have. Every week at the *Sentinel* meetings. And you. Don't. Listen. I figured it would be quicker to come and let you see for yourself than argue over it."

"I listen."

"But you don't hear."

I walked to the escalator, and he followed me. "I don't even know what that means."

He laughed. "It's exactly this: You don't like what someone says and you walk away. There's no real discussion. You make up your mind, and it doesn't matter what the other person thinks."

"That is not true." I turned to face him as we made our way down to the lower level. "I listen to Morgan."

"Do you? Or does she just tell you what you want to hear?"

I was fuming. How dare he?! Morgan was my best friend. Of

course I listened to her and valued her opinions. "You don't know what you're talking about. Morgan and—"

"Charlie!"

"No, don't you *Charlie* me, I—"

"Charlie!!" he raised his voice.

So typical. Here he was talking over me while claiming *I* was the one who didn't listen.

"Watch it!" he yelled and reached out to grab my arm. Only it was too late. I had reached the bottom of the escalator. And seeing as I wasn't paying any attention and was facing the wrong direction, I completely lost my footing. I stumbled back. *Oh no, oh no, oh no.* I tried to steady myself, but I had too much momentum going. I couldn't stop myself. I backed right into someone. "Careful," they hissed, shoving me away. And it wasn't a light shove; it was hard enough to send me flying forward, right to the left of the escalator. Right into a display of about two dozen poinsettia plants set up to look like a Christmas tree.

I covered my head with my arms as dirt and flowers and pots rained down on my head.

"Whoa," J.D. said, rushing over. "Are you"—he was clearly trying to hold back a laugh—"okay?"

The jerk was smiling. He was biting his lower lip, but the corners of his mouth were unmistakably drawn upward.

"This is not funny," I said, brushing the dirt off my coat. Six of the plants had fallen.

"Not at all," he said, while totally letting out several snickers. "Sorry. I really don't mean to laugh." He held out his hand for me to take.

I pushed it away. "I don't need your help."

My little stunt had attracted a crowd.

"Nothing to see here, people," J.D. called out while still enjoying his laughing fit. "Go shop. Christmas is coming." A couple of people still lingered, totally enjoying my humiliation.

I tried to hide my face from them all. "Stop laughing," I told J.D., but of course he didn't. "You're totally getting coal for Christmas," I warned him. Although as I looked at the mess surrounding me, I did have to fight back a laugh or two of my own. But I wasn't going to let J.D. know that. "Stupid poinsettias," I muttered instead as I started picking them up and putting them back on their stand.

"Well, it's not really the plants' fault, now is it?" J.D. asked.

J.D., who now had his camera out and aimed straight at me!

"WHAT ARE YOU DOING?!! Put that away. J.D., I am serious. Stop taking pictures."

"Oh, this is great, keep waving the poinsettia at me."

"J.D. . . ."

"This one is going to looking really good in the *Sentinel* spread. Maybe I won't even use any other pictures. Maybe it will just be this one giant image of you."

"You are not putting this in the paper," I told him.

"Wait. Who has control of this issue? I think that's me," he said as he moved to the other side to get a different angle.

I picked up the last plant and scooped up as much dirt as I could. "The deal is off."

"Yeah," J.D. said. "That's not how deals work. Besides, I've already come up with your first gift for Teo, and it won't cost you a cent."

"Let me guess," I said. "A picture of me looking like a fool?"

"Nah." J.D. shook his head. "It's *Secret* Santa, remember? And it wouldn't be fair to share this picture with just one person when it could bring joy to so many. These pictures should be for the *whole* student body to enjoy, don't you agree?"

Jerk, jerk, jerk, jerk, jerk. "I swear," I said, "I should just leave you here."

"That's fair," he said. "But then you'd never get the Teo gift I was talking about. I'll only tell you after you drop me off."

I seriously wanted to throttle him. Or at least tell him what he could do with his gift idea. But after all this, there was no way I wasn't getting that present. I'd come too far to back out now. "Fine. Let's go."

When we got back to my car, I looked in the rearview mirror. Dirt was smeared on my face and a red poinsettia petal was stuck in my hair. J.D. picked it out and handed it to me.

I waved it off. "I'm over poinsettias. My new least favorite Christmas decoration."

"But look how nicely they photograph." He pulled out his camera and turned the viewer toward me, which revealed a pic of me surrounded by all of the plants on the ground.

I just glared at him.

My look must have spoken volumes, because it was enough to keep J.D. from opening his mouth the rest of the ride to his house.

"So what is this brainstorm gift idea of yours, which you could have told me about before I made a fool of myself at the mall but decided to wait until now?" I asked as I parked in front of his house.

"A playlist," he said matter-of-factly.

"*That's* your big idea? And tell me, just how do I transfer this playlist to him without giving away my identity?"

"Ever hear of a thumb drive?"

Duh. Of course. I could just save the files there, and Teo could transfer them to his phone later. "Okay, fine. Just pick out some songs he'll like and throw them on the drive. You can get it to me tomorrow or Tuesday. I'm planning on giving him the first gift Wednesday."

"Wait, wait, wait." J.D. held up his hands. "Is this a gift from me, or a gift from you? Don't you think you should have a hand in picking out the songs?"

He did have a point, and I was curious about Teo's taste in music.

"Come on in," he said. "It won't take that long."

But I couldn't. I had hit my threshold of how much J.D. Ortiz I could handle in one day. "Not tonight."

"Tuesday after school?" he asked.

"That works. And don't forget you're supposed to be helping me spend time with Teo, too."

"I remember," he mumbled.

"Good," I shouted out my window as J.D. walked to his door. Because right now, I was spending way too much time with the wrong Ortiz cousin. And that definitely needed to change.

Twelve

Monday and most of the day Tuesday, to my disappointment, I had no contact with Teo, and to my delight, just small interactions with J.D. He and I had world history and study hall together, but I did my best to avoid him.

By the looks of things, the newspaper staff had begun to get their holiday surprises. "Guess what my Secret Santa got me!" Morgan said, waving some sort of stuffed animal at me as I left last period. Her class was right across from mine. "It was waiting on my desk."

"What is that thing?"

"It's a stuffed dreidel." Only it had big googly eyes and accordion legs. "And look at this . . ." She squeezed it, and it started playing "I Have a Little Dreidel."

"Okay, that is one of the corniest things I've ever seen."

"I know, right?" she said. "That's why I love it."

Only Morgan would get that excited over a silly toy. "It's better than what I got." I pulled out a candy cane that was broken in three pieces. "I found it before last period. They jammed it in the slit of my locker with a note that said *Merry Christmas, Secret Santa.*"

"Well, at least they were thinking about you, and it's the thought that counts, right?"

"Okay, Pollyanna," I said. "I think they just took the candy cane from the jar in the main office."

"So what?" she said. "Some people haven't gotten anything yet." That was true. I hadn't given Teo a present. I was meeting J.D. in twenty minutes to go over the first gift. "Your Secret Santa may be just warming up. I wonder who it is?"

"No idea, but I guess we solved the mystery of who's your Secret Santa." There was just one person from the paper in her last-period class.

"It's not necessarily Gus," she said as we headed to our lockers. "Someone else could have snuck in and done it or asked him to help them out."

"I think you are giving the people on our staff way too much credit. Besides, if someone was trying to be stealthy, they wouldn't ask Gus." Gus was nice and all, and he even managed to come up with some good story ideas, but his lack of attention to the not-so-little things like spelling and grammar made me cringe. He definitely wasn't the person I would turn to for help.

"Well, I don't care," she declared. "At least he's trying." She squeezed the stuffed dreidel again. "And I think this is adorable."

"What's adorable?" Ira asked, coming up from behind.

"Oh, just another guy trying to woo me with presents."

"Cool," he said. "Does that mean I don't have to get you anything?"

She hit him lightly with her new gift. "It doesn't mean that at all."

He put his arm around her and pulled her closer as we continued to walk. She did the same to him.

When we stopped at her locker, Ira was moving the hair off of the back of her neck as she put her books away. "Okay, I'm leaving," I said, before they started making out or something.

Before I had a chance to make my getaway, Noelle Hawkins stopped in front of me, her arms crossed over her chest. "You have not RSVP'd to my party."

"Oh, hey, Noelle. It's still a couple of weeks away," I argued. "We practically just got the invitation."

"But you've known about it forever. And Morgan and Ira still found time to RSVP. So did most people."

Noelle and I weren't amazingly close, but she was one of the few people in this school, other than Morgan and Ira, that I actually called a friend. We had a shared camaraderie over birthdays on major holidays. We commiserated about it on more than one occasion.

I looked down at my feet. "I'm still trying to figure out if I can go."

"What are you talking about? Why wouldn't you?" she asked.

Because I wasn't sure if my Teo plan would be successful or not, and I wasn't going to her mistletoe-infested holiday extravaganza without a date. But I couldn't really tell her that.

Not that she gave me a chance to answer. She just kept right on talking. "I already have you down for a tentative yes. With Ajay as your plus-one. You need to be there. You never mentioned not coming. This is going to be *the* party of the year. You are not missing my birthday. Besides, the theme is Lovers' Ball, and while I know you and Ajay are just friends now," she said, her voice getting all singsongy, "this party could change all that. And don't tell me you're not secretly hoping to get back together."

"Yeah, about that, Ajay and I aren't really talking anymore," I confessed.

"Wait, what?!" She looked more upset than I did about it. "Okay, this isn't a disaster." Although her expression was telling me that it was. I knew she was all about the couple thing, but come on. Not that I was *that* surprised. When Noelle had an idea in her head, she stuck to it, which I both respected and, at the moment, hated. "We can fix this," she said, her tone getting serious. "I'll find you a date. You can take one of my cousins. One of the twins. Your choice."

"The twins? The ones who've been at your party every single year? Aren't they like fourteen?"

"Yeah, well," she hemmed, "if you had told me sooner, I would have saved one of the older ones for you, but I already matched all of them up."

"I am not going to your party with a freshman."

"What's this I hear?" Zakiyah said, sidling up to me.

Seriously? TMZ needed to give this girl a job. It was like she had a sixth sense for where there was dirt to be found.

"No one was talking to you," I said, taking a step away.

"Yeah, but I wouldn't be doing my job as the paper's gossip columnist if I didn't check into everything. And you know, I have, like, the most annoying editor, so I better do my due diligence." She gave me an evil grin. "So tell me, does someone not have a date anymore? I guess you'll just be a poor, sorry loser then."

"What is wrong with you?" Morgan interrupted her. "Not having a date does not make you a loser. In fact, the whole idea of needing one is ridiculous."

"Hey!" Noelle said.

Morgan cringed. "No offense."

"Oh, don't look at me," Zakiyah said. "They're not *my* words, right, Charlie? And just to help me clarify, I was right before, huh? You were dumped? Did he get sick of your self-righteousness, or was it the way you have to have every little thing planned so it goes your way? Because, personally, I'd find them both pretty annoying."

"Whatever, Zakiyah," I said.

"Great comeback." She turned to Noelle. "Anyway, good luck finding her a date, 'cause, wow, you are going to need it."

I don't know if it was the smug look of satisfaction on her face or the tone of her voice or that she managed to push my last button, but before I could stop myself, I was up in her face. "I'll have you know, I ended it with Ajay, because I moved on. I'll be at Noelle's party *as a couple*. And just wait until you see my date. He's perfect. He's going to be the best one there."

Then I flicked my hair over my shoulder and walked to my locker.

No, no, no, no, no, no, no, no, no.

Why hadn't I kept my big mouth shut?

Now Operation Secret Santa had to work. There was absolutely no room for failure. My reputation depended on it.

Thirteen

Y ou know," J.D. said when I got to his house. "If you were coming here anyway, you could have given me a ride home instead of letting me walk."

"Oh, sorry." It hadn't even crossed my mind. Ira usually drove Morgan, and I didn't even think about how J.D. got back and forth to school. It wasn't like we were friends.

"That's okay. It's all about you, right?"

First Zakiyah and now J.D.? He may have been joking, but it sure didn't feel like it, and I had had enough for one day. "First of all," I informed him, "you could have asked. How was I supposed to know you needed a ride? So don't put that on me."

"You're right," he acquiesced, but I wasn't through with him. I was so sick of people like him assuming I only thought about myself because I voiced my opinions and wasn't constantly worried about being a people pleaser.

"Second," I continued, "you are getting just as much out of this deal as I am, so don't even start. You are such a—"

Then I remembered where I was and slapped my hand over my mouth. I wouldn't want my mom hearing someone bash me, especially in my own home. J.D. watched me look around.

"Don't worry. It's just us. My sister's still up at college, and my parents—*Teo's* aunt and uncle—are at work."

Yeah, yeah, he didn't need to point it out. I remembered he was related to Teo and could make or break whether I got my Lovers' Ball date or not.

I let out a sigh. "Are we going to make this playlist or not?"

"Follow me," he said.

We went upstairs. He turned into the room right off to the left and stopped short. "We can actually work on it downstairs if you prefer. I can bring my laptop down."

"Why?" I said, sneaking a look past him into his bedroom. "Did you forget to clean or something? Don't worry about it. I already assumed you were a slob."

"No . . . I just thought you might be more com—Forget it."

Then it hit me what he meant. He was worried I wouldn't feel comfortable being alone with him in his room. I studied his face. That was actually nice of him. Every so often he did something that surprised me. But there was nothing to worry about. I didn't look at him in any sort of romantic way. The idea of kissing J.D. Ortiz was about as appealing as taking a nap on the bathroom floor. And while I might have thought of him as a pompous, unprepared, pigheaded jerk, I felt safe around him. Being in his room was no big deal.

He stepped aside from the door, and I went in. It was not what I expected at all. "It's so neat."

"Okay, why do you think I'm such a slob?"

"Do you really want to know?"

"Please," he said, and gestured for me to take a seat at his desk.

"Just remember that you asked," I said as I sat down in the chair. "You're never on time, you always seem to be in a rush, your bag is filled with papers that a neat person would have in a binder, and your hair goes in a hundred different directions— but not in that I'm-trying-to-look-like-I-didn't-work-on-this-for-hours-but-actually-did way, but in the actual I-woke-up-this-way way. Plus, look at your shoelace—it's untied again—and then there all those studies that say creative people are messier in general, and you always claim to have artistic vision. So, I'd say thinking you were a slob would be a reasonable hypothesis."

He let out a low whistle.

"It's not like being a slob is horrible," I explained after seeing the stunned look on his face. "Morgan's room is a disaster, and she's one of the smartest people I've met." Morgan may have loved reality TV and spending most of her free time baking and with her boyfriend, but she was also kind of a math genius. Enough so that she breezed through calculus our sophomore year and now spent her math period taking an online college-level course in topology, which dealt with geometric properties and spatial relations. Yet when it came to her bedroom, it looked like someone ransacked it. I found myself straightening things up when we were in there, which drove her nuts. As a result, we mostly hung out in her den or kitchen when we were at her house.

"But I'm not a slob!" J.D. protested.

"Okay." I raised my hands. "I can see that. Don't get so defensive. You're very neat. There, happy now? I don't know why you're getting so upset."

"Because you have this messed-up view of me."

Why did he care what I thought? "Because you make my job as an editor harder."

"I make you better."

"Let's just start the playlist, please." I did not want to get into another argument with him.

"Fine. I'm going to go grab another chair."

While he was gone, I studied the setup of his room. It was actually pretty impressive. He had a long, white tabletop desk that was almost the length of one of the walls. There were two giant monitors on top, a printer, a sketch pad, and a cup that held pens, paper clips, and such. He also had a bunch of little plastic models, which I'm guessing he'd made on the 3-D printer at his internship, and there were heaping stacks of photos that took over the far left side of the desk. Another wall consisted of just bookshelves, and they were filled with actual books. I hadn't taken him for a reader, but after the way he reacted to me thinking he was a slob, I certainly wasn't going to share that opinion. The third wall was all windows, with deep-blue curtains, and up against the fourth was his bed and a little nightstand. Framed photos were overhead.

J.D. returned with a bridge chair and placed it next to me. "Ready for the musical stylings of Teo?"

Was I ever.

"Then get ready to visit the eighties."

"The what?" I asked.

"The eighties."

"Ha-ha," I said. "What does he really like?"

"I'm being serious," J.D. said, holding his fingers up in the Boy Scout pledge.

He had to be kidding. "Really?"

"Why would I lie?" he asked.

"I don't know why you do a lot of things," I said. "To mess with me because you think it's funny, because—"

"I don't need another one of your lists," he said, half laughing. "I get it, but I promise you, Teo loves the eighties."

"*Why?*" I mean, I'm sure the decade had its moments, but that's the type of stuff my mother listens to. If Teo was going to pick something old, why not some old-time jazz or the Beatles or *anything* else?

"There are some decent songs from back then," J.D. said, coming to his cousin's defense.

"I know, but it's his *favorite*? I just don't get it."

"You'll have to ask him."

That idea made me smile. I may not have loved eighties music the way Teo did, but getting to know him better sounded really good. And after what went down with Zakiyah, a necessity.

"I have no idea what songs to pick," I confessed. "Honestly, I'm kind of musically illiterate."

"That's hard to believe."

"No, it's true. I shouldn't be making fun of Teo. I know

83

nothing about music. I can sing along to a ton of songs, but if you ask me who sang them or what they're called, I'm hopeless."

"That doesn't surprise me at all," he said, punching something up on the computer. Then he turned to me. His eyes had a little glint to them. "The surprise was you admitting you actually don't know something."

I smacked him in the arm. "Such a comedian."

"Admit it, I'm growing on you."

"I plead the Fifth. After all, I still need your help."

"Look who's funny now," he said. "Here, these are the songs my dad has on his iPhone. There's a ton of eighties stuff."

"Do you know which ones Teo already has?" I asked.

"Nope," he said. "But does it really matter? The idea is to show him that you took an interest in what he likes. You don't have to nail each song."

"That's true, and it will definitely be better than what I got today." I pulled the candy cane from my bag. "Pre-crushed and all."

"Wait, that's what . . ." J.D. stopped talking.

"What?"

"Sorry, just got distracted by the files," he said, and started punching some random keys on the computer.

"Are you okay?" He was acting weird, almost a little shady. "Were you the one who gave me the candy cane?"

"No! I am a good gift giver, remember? Besides, I drew Katie's name," J.D. said, still playing with the computer.

I scanned the titles of his dad's music on the screen closest to me. There were a lot of them. "Truthfully, I don't really care what I get. For me this is about Teo." I rubbed my temples as I continued to peruse the never-ending eighties song choices. "I seriously have no idea what to put on this playlist. Can we just take the ten your dad listens to the most?"

"Charlie Donovan, are you suggesting taking a shortcut?" J.D. asked in mock disgust. "Cheating, even?"

"It's not cheating. It's taking advice from an expert, in this case, your dad," I explained.

"All right, if your conscience can live with it. But I do think we need to put this one as track number one," he said, and punched up a song. "This is what you live by, right?"

The lyric "It's hip to be square" filled the room.

"Huey Lewis and the News," he informed me. "I think it sums you up."

"Me? Fine, maybe I am a square or a nerd or whatever. But who are you to talk? Don't think I didn't notice some of those books on your shelves." I stood up and pointed to *Hellenistic Art: From Alexander the Great to Augustus* and *National Geographic Image Collection*. I put on my best grandma voice, "Are these what all the kids are reading these days?"

"I own my geek status proudly," he said. "And they're not all nonfiction. I read everything."

I studied his shelves as the music files transferred onto the drive. He really did have eclectic taste. There were a bunch of art and photography books, but there were also biographies of everyone from world leaders to stand-up comedians, history books, mysteries, horror novels, and even some rom-coms. I loved books, but lately I'd been reading more articles and studies. Looking at his never-ending shelves kind of made me crave reading something with more meat to it.

He must have seen me salivating because he said, "You can borrow one if you want."

"What do you recommend?"

He moved to the third shelf by the window. "I think these are fitting. Welcome to my Christmas selections."

"You have a whole shelf of Christmas books?"

J.D. pulled out a book. "Don't say it like it's a bad thing."

"I'm not. I'm just surprised."

"I'm all about Christmas," he said, and handed me the book. "This will put you in the holiday mood. It's a play on Scrooge, but told by the Ghost of Christmas Past, who accidentally alters history and then has to work with the Ghost of Christmas Present and the Ghost of Christmas Future to save everyone's Christmas." J.D. paused and put his arms out. "Did the Earth stop rotating?"

"Huh?" I asked.

"It's just, I figured something big had to have happened. You look as if you may actually like my suggestion."

Like and *J.D.* did not belong in the same sentence, but I had to admit it sounded like a fun book. "You are ridiculous," I said, and put the book in my bag.

"Only in the best way, though, right?"

"You are not getting me to compliment you."

He took the flash drive out of the computer. "Not even after I give you this?"

I took it and held it close to my chest. "Okay, yes, you are amazing. Well, *this* is amazing anyway."

It really was. Thanks to J.D., tomorrow Teo was going to get his first Secret Santa gift, and I was going to be on my way to proving to Zakiyah, myself, and the world that I could win the heart of the most perfect guy on the planet.

Fourteen

I set my alarm ten minutes earlier than usual so I could ensure I'd be at school before Teo. But I didn't have to bother. I was so anxious about everything working out right that I could barely sleep. I was up way before my alarm sounded.

Today was a two-part plan. First the delivery of the gift, and then running into Teo. I put the flash drive in an envelope. I had spent an hour going back and forth on the note. I thought about using the names of some of the songs that were on the drive in an attempt to be flirty: *"Don't You Want Me"* to be your Secret Santa? *"Sweet Dreams (Are Made of This)"* . . . *and finding out who is giving you these gifts. "Karma Chameleon" is bringing us together.* But I was smart enough to realize how totally corny that sounded. So I kept it simple. A track list, and for the signature, I didn't want to write *"Love,* your Secret Santa," so I just put a heart instead. Then I taped it to his locker.

Then I waited for part two—the "accidental" meeting. It took a little snooping, but I managed to get Teo's schedule. I compared it with mine, and it seemed the best time to catch him was after last period. Our classrooms were in the same hallway, and there was no bell to rush us along—but it was still risky. If he booked it to his car before I made it out, or if he made a surprise detour to the water fountain instead of the main entrance, I could miss him and have to wait another day to talk to him. I didn't like leaving things to chance, and with so many variables to account for, I made this my backup plan.

Which meant that plan A was after my fourth-period world history class. This was a little trickier—and would rely on luck—which was not something I liked to count on. After fourth period was when Teo headed to lunch. According to my estimation, if he headed straight to the cafeteria within a minute or two of the bell ringing, he'd pass my class, we'd have a chance to talk, and I'd still make it to fifth period on time. BUT if he went to his locker first, I'd have to resort to plan B. Teo's locker was all the way in the senior hallway, which was in the opposite direction of my class. And as much as I wanted to talk to him, I did not want to be late to fifth period.

Normally, my hand was the first one up during all my classes, but today I couldn't concentrate. All I could think about was what I was going to say to Teo. I couldn't risk sounding like a fool, so I did some prep work. I was now prepared to speak with him about the newspaper, his Secret Santa gift, eighties music (which I spent a few hours researching last night), his volunteering, and even the football game. I watched the clock tick toward the 11:30

mark. Every second felt like minutes. With just thirty seconds to go, I crossed my fingers and prayed that Teo would be where I needed him to be. As soon as the bell rang, I bolted for the door. I didn't want to risk missing him walk by. A minute passed. Then another. My whole body was heating up. This had to work. *Come on, Teo.* I couldn't wait much longer.

"Let me guess what you're doing," a voice said from behind me.

I didn't need to look to know it was J.D. "Don't start," I warned him.

Not that it mattered. J.D. was going to be J.D. regardless of what I told him. "Oh, I hope he comes by," he said, in what I'm assuming was his best impression of me, even though my voice was nowhere near that high or squeaky. Then he put his hand on his forehead. "Look, it's him! I may just faint."

He might have been joking, but he was right about Teo heading our way.

J.D. shook his head. "Your eyes seriously popped out like a cartoon character's. You need to rein it in," he said. "What's next? Will your heart beat a foot from your chest, or maybe you'll actually melt into the floor?"

I ignored him and instead summoned all my courage and waved his cousin over. "Teo," I called out.

I could feel my heartbeat quicken. I had actually done it. I was going to talk to Teo Ortiz. Everything was going to plan. Well, except for the fact that J.D. was standing there. He was not part of the equation. "Go," I whispered.

He didn't move. He was enjoying watching me squirm.

Right as Teo approached, J.D. decided to speak up. "What's that, Charlie? Do you want me to leave so you can be alone with—"

I elbowed him in the side. Why did he have to be so annoying?

"Teo," I said, following the script I carefully crafted. "I'm so glad you were able to make it to the *Sentinel* meeting last week. We can definitely use someone like you on the paper."

"Definitely," J.D. said, mocking me.

I was not going to let him get me off track. I was nervous enough as it was, which was why I had practiced what I was going to say about six dozen times. There was no way I was going to stumble over my words in front of Teo. I had done my homework.

"Thanks," he said, and gave me one of his dazzling smiles. It was one of those that went all the way up to his eyes. His amazing dark eyes that I needed to stop focusing on so I could keep speaking.

"Did you get anything from your Secret Santa?" I asked, and reminded myself to smile back at him.

"A playlist of songs," he said.

I couldn't read his expression. Did he like the gift? Did he hate my song choices? I had planned responses in both instances, but none for apathy.

"That sounds nice," I said, leading him in the direction I was hoping for.

"Yeah," he said noncommittally.

"What kind of songs?" I asked.

"Bunch of oldies." He moved his bag to his other shoulder and looked toward the cafeteria.

Oh no. I was boring him. This was not how it was supposed to go. He was supposed to be flirty and help spur the conversation forward. Instead he was looking for an exit strategy. *Think, Charlie. Think! Go with football.*

"You have a big game coming up on Friday, right?"

"*The* game," he answered, the sparkle coming back into his eye. "Win this and the championship is ours."

"I know you guys will be amazing. Your record is impeccable."

"You're going to be there cheering him on, right?" J.D. butted in.

Thanks a lot, J.D. He knew I wasn't into sports. I didn't like watching games on TV, and I certainly didn't like having to watch them while sitting outside in the freezing cold. But now I had no choice.

"Of course I'll be there," I said. I was going to kill J.D. for this later. "Wouldn't miss it."

"I'll keep my eye out for you," Teo said and smiled at me.

My breathing picked up. He was going to look out—for *me*? Okay, maybe J.D. hadn't had such a bad idea after all. This was a step in the right direction.

The warning bell rang, and I knew I should go, but I didn't want to. Teo motioned toward the cafeteria with a little nod of his head and started walking. I followed, and so did his cousin.

"You should join us after the game," J.D. said. "A bunch of us are going to Scobell's."

"Yeah?" I asked. J.D. may have done the inviting, but I directed my question toward Teo. "I wouldn't be intruding?"

"Of course not," Teo said and winked at me. "You should definitely come."

"I'll be there," I said.

Teo turned into the cafeteria, and I just stood there watching him disappear into the crowd.

You should definitely come. And a wink. I was making progress. This was good. Better than good.

"Don't say I haven't been holding up my end of the bargain," J.D. said, interrupting my thoughts. "I got you your 'Teo time.'"

"So far, so good," I said. Secretly I was jumping up and down. He had done an awesome job, but I wasn't quite ready to admit that to his face.

The bell rang, and I cut off my conversation with J.D.

My love life was finally headed in the right direction, but that still wasn't an excuse to be late. I raced down the hall. Schedules and plans were meant to be followed. It's how I was going to win over Teo Ortiz, and so far, everything was going like clockwork.

Fifteen

"We could have snuck in right at the end of the game, or at the very least at intermission," Morgan said as we maneuvered into the stands at the football field.

"You mean halftime," I corrected her. I might have known next to nothing about sports, but Morgan actually knew *nothing*.

"Whatever it's called, I don't care, we could have come then. Someone would have filled us in on what we missed," she said. "Teo wouldn't know if we were actually here or not."

"Weren't you the one who told me I was an awful liar and shouldn't do it?"

"Wellllll . . ." She shrugged. "That was before I knew it entailed me sitting through an entire football game on cold metal bleachers."

"It's not exactly on my bucket list either, but thank you for coming with me," I said, and tried breathing into my hands to generate a little extra warmth. Even with gloves, a giant puffy coat, a hat, and a scarf on, it was freezing.

"Yeah, yeah," she said and pulled out her thermos filled with hot tea. "You owe me."

"Hey, what happened to Miss School Spirit? You're usually into things like this," I reminded her.

"I like Secret Santas and parties and the school paper and the Math Bowl. Things that don't involve me turning into a Popsicle."

"Well, I will buy you whatever you want at Scobell's afterward to make up for it."

"Fine," she said and began rocking for warmth.

I let out a groan.

"What?" she asked.

"Look to your left."

Making his way over to us was J.D. *Ugh.* "Like I haven't had enough of him this week?"

"Be nice," she warned me. "He's helping you, and if it wasn't for him, you wouldn't be hanging out with Teo after the game, and we wouldn't be here. If anyone should be mad, it should be me! All I'm getting out of this is a milkshake."

"And helping a friend," I reminded her.

"Yes, and helping a friend," she repeated back.

"Well, well, well," J.D. said, taking a seat behind us, and putting one arm over Morgan's shoulder and one arm over mine. "If it isn't my favorite neighbor and her number two."

"Number *one*," I said, and flicked his arm off me. I didn't do second place.

"I bet Ira would beg to differ. Where is he anyway?"

Morgan shook her head at us. She was used to J.D. and me egging each other on. It had been this way since the beginning of the year when she and I took over as coeditors. "Ira does Friday night dinner with his family. He's going to meet us at the diner afterward."

"Shouldn't you be taking pictures?" I asked him, in a not-so-subtle attempt to remind him of his newspaper duties *and* to get him to leave us alone.

"Roger's helping out. He's down there," J.D. answered. "I thought I'd get some shots from up here, a more *artsy* take, just the way you like it."

"Are you trying to make me hate you?" I asked.

"*Trying*," he said. "That means you don't. See, I knew I was moving up in your eyes."

"I think you missed the operative word in my sentence."

"Me? You?" he tried.

"Hate."

He took an imaginary dagger and stabbed his heart. "You're killing me. And just when I had the perfect gift idea for you too."

"Yeah, what?" I asked.

J.D. pretended to zip his lips.

"What, you're turning into a mime now? Just tell me."

He shook his head.

"Come on," I insisted.

He made some garbled noises, keeping up his ridiculous lips-sealed routine.

"I'm serious, J.D.," I said. When he didn't answer, I turned away from him and took a deep breath. I was not going to let him ruin this night for me. It was already bad enough being stuck outside watching a sporting event I knew nothing about.

"Okay," he said. "I'll tell you."

When I turned back around, he said, "Just kidding."

"I swear I'm—"

"Both of you stop, please," Morgan said. "Even watching this game is more appealing than watching you two fight. I can't take a whole night of it."

We both mumbled an apology.

The game had started, and we all sat quietly watching. After a few minutes, Morgan whispered, "Which one is Teo?"

The truth was, I had no idea. We were far enough away that I couldn't make out faces. It just looked like a mess of bodies dressed in white and red bashing into other bodies dressed in yellow and blue.

I could hear J.D. shooting pictures behind me. He would know the answer. I decided to suck it up. If I had to watch the game, I might as well watch the guy that I came there to see. "Can you please tell me which one is Teo?" I asked, trying my best to be polite.

"By the goalpost," he said. "Number ten."

His number I knew. After all, it was fitting. If anyone was a ten at Sandbrook High, it was Teo. I just couldn't make out the numbers on the shirts.

"Here, look," he said, holding his camera out so I could see in the display. It was zoomed in on the field, and J.D. moved it so I got a clear look at Teo. I almost felt like I could reach out and touch him. Teo looked so intense out there. So disciplined. So focused. It's part of what I loved about him. He knew what he wanted, went for it, and got it.

"Whoa, whoa." J.D. stood up, camera in hand. "Do you see that!?"

I saw Teo, but I wasn't sure what was happening.

J.D. was snapping pictures. "Go, Teo," he screamed.

"Wait, what's going on?" I asked.

"Your boy just threw a sixty-yard pass, and they got it all the way to the one yard line."

Morgan and I started cheering with everyone else in the crowd.

"Maybe this isn't so bad," she said.

She was right, the enthusiasm was sort of contagious.

By halftime, my throat was sore from cheering so loud for Teo, who, if I understood correctly, had jumped over the line and scored a touchdown, putting his team in the lead.

"I never thought I'd like a football game," I said. I guess it helped having someone to root for.

"See what happens when you try something new?" J.D. said as he stood up and stretched.

"Well, that wasn't condescending at all," I informed him.

"You're right," he said. "To make it up to you, I won't make you wait to find out my next gift idea."

"I'm listening," I said.

"Jim Dandies."

"Jim who?"

"They're cookies," he said. "Amazing cookies. Our aunt used

to make them at Christmastime when we were little, but she hasn't done it in years. They were always Teo's favorites. Mine, too."

"I've never heard of them," Morgan said.

"They're really good. They're fudgy, frosted, with a little marshmallow hidden underneath and a cherry on top."

"Do you have the recipe?" Morgan asked. "I can make them for you to give," she told me.

"Are you sure? It's my gift. I don't want to cause you more work."

"I really don't mind. And you did say you wanted to *impress* him, not *poison* him," she pointed out.

"Nice," I said, laughing. "Ye of little faith. Have you seen the science experiments I've worked on? I've dealt with NaOH for titration and never ended up with burns. I used the right amount of sodium hydroxide and neutralized it with hydrochloric acid to produce sodium chloride, and that was one of my easier tasks. I've never overheated a Pyrex tube. I've never caused an explosion. I've never—"

"I know, I know," she said, stopping me, a huge grin on her face. "That's why it's so perplexing that you can't make a simple cookie. But trust me, I've seen the final products."

"It's not my fault," I complained. "You know how some people have bad computer karma, where the modem seems to magically crash or stop working for no reason when they are around? That's me and cooking."

"Which is why I will make the cookies for you," she said.

"Thank you! You are the best," I told her.

"Her?" J.D. asked. "It was my idea."

I rolled my eyes at him, and Morgan shook her head again. "Look," she said, and pointed at the side of the stadium. The team was coming back from the locker room.

"Now's your chance," J.D. said.

"For what?"

"To let Teo know that you're here."

"Are you crazy?" I asked.

He shrugged. "I thought you wanted him to notice you?"

I did. And Teo did say he'd look out for me. Standing and hollering out to him while everyone else was relatively quiet would definitely help him find me. But it would also draw a lot of unwanted attention. Still, sometimes getting what you wanted meant getting out of your comfort zone. I had no choice. Noelle's party was fast approaching.

I jumped up and yelled, "Go, Teo!"

My voice permeated the air. Everyone around me turned to look.

I sank into my seat.

Okay, maybe it wasn't such a smart idea after all. *Or* maybe it was. Because just then Teo looked up and waved. I was pretty sure he knew it was me. I waved back.

This was going just the way I needed it to. Teo might have been the one winning the game, but right now it felt like I was, too.

Sixteen

Ira showed up at Scobell's Diner about two minutes after we got there. The staff was still setting up a large table for us in the back. He gave Morgan a quick kiss. "Who won?"

"Can't you tell?" she asked.

Standing not even three feet away from us was a sizeable chunk of the football team. They were slapping each other's backs, talking in incredibly loud voices, and acting extremely hyped up.

"CHAMP-I-ONS! CHAMP-I-ONS! CHAMP-I-ONS!" they chanted for the third time in mere minutes. Only now they were even drumming on the walls for added effect. Fortunately for the restaurant, everyone there seemed to have just come from the game, so they didn't seem to mind the craziness.

"I think I figured it out," Ira said.

"What gave it away?" I asked.

The waitress came over and told us all—well, those of us who could hear her over the shouting—that there was a large table set up in the back, and the rest of us could take the surrounding booths.

I looked over at Teo. Two of his teammates had him up on their shoulders and they were walking around the diner, letting him high-five everyone. The whole point of coming out was to spend time with him, but how was I supposed to score a seat near the boy wonder? He led the team to victory; they won thirty-five to seven, and Teo was responsible for almost every point. He was the star; everyone was going to want to be near him. He was bound to sit at the center of the table, and I couldn't very well take the seat next to him, could I?

Talking to Teo was the only reason I came here. My goal was to have a solid five-minute conversation with him tonight, but as I pulled out a chair at the head table, I knew I didn't belong there. "Maybe we should take a booth." It felt weird intruding on the celebration. His friends would definitely say something about the random juniors who knew nothing about sports crashing their celebration. That's not how I wanted Teo to think of me.

"Where are you going?" J.D. asked as Morgan, Ira, and I passed him. He was leaning against some old arcade game in the back corner.

"We're going to go sit over there." I pointed to a side booth.

"No, you're not. Come on," J.D. said, and he gestured for us to follow him. He brought us back to the main table. "I need some pictures for the paper," he called out to the room. He pointed to the seat across from him in the center. "I want Teo to sit there with the starting lineup on that side. I'll sit over here and get some candids of everyone." Then he looked at me. "You and your friends can sit here, too."

I felt a rush of relief wash over me. "Thank you," I mouthed to him.

He nodded. Then half to himself, half to me, he muttered, "I really should have asked for control of the photos for the whole year."

He absolutely should have, but lucky for me, he didn't.

I took the seat next to where J.D. was standing, and Morgan took my other side. I'd be diagonal from Teo, not directly facing him, but that was okay. I read a study that said sitting right across from someone was a setup for confrontation, and I obviously didn't want a fight. Preferably, he'd look at me and think how smart and amazingly easy I was to talk to.

As Teo was paraded back to the table, J.D. took pictures and said, "You're right there."

Teo took his seat, and I couldn't help but stare. He looked so happy, so confident, so proud. He had the look of a winner. That was definitely the type of guy for me.

"Congratulations," I said. "You were incredible."

"He's the BEAST!" Reggie Weeks, another player on the team, yelled out. Then the whole team yelled, "The BEAST!"

If Teo was letting it all go to his head, he didn't show it. He bowed his head slightly and then looked up at me through his long lashes. "Thanks. Glad you could make it."

Don't hyperventilate, don't hyperventilate. "Wouldn't miss it."

I kicked myself for not studying up on the intricacies of football more. It would have been a better use of my time than the eighties music, but I could improvise. What had J.D. said earlier? "That touchdown you made at the start of the game was unbelievable. That you could go sixty yards and get the team to the one yard line, majorly impressive."

I could feel J.D. looking at me. Yes, I stole his words, but they say imitation is the sincerest form of flattery. Hopefully, he would take it that way anyway and not call me out.

"It was a great way to end the season, and my high school football career," Teo said, smiling.

I loved that smile. Warm and inviting. Not like J.D.'s—smug and irritating.

"Are you going to play in college?" I asked him, grateful for something I knew how to talk about. I could rattle on about anything related to school for hours.

"Maybe. I'm still figuring it out. I got a couple of offers, but I also got a few academic scholarships, too. If I want to go the pre-med route, I don't know if I'll have time to play."

"It's hard to find time for everything. But you're doing it now, volunteering at the hospital and playing."

"True," he said, "but college will be a whole different level. And I just don't know what I want more. You know?"

"I do. That's a tough—"

"You gonna order or what?" Reggie asked him, interrupting us.

I had been so engrossed in our conversation, I hadn't even noticed the waitress standing over him.

But it seemed I wasn't the only one who felt that way. The normally cool, calm, and collected Teo stammered over his words. "Um, yeah, sorry." Then he looked at me and smiled again.

A wave of warmth went through me. There *was* something between us. Teo had to have felt it, too. It was almost as if there had been a spell over us, wiping away everyone else at the table. Unfortunately, Reggie managed to break it.

He hijacked Teo into his conversation as the rest of us told the waitress what we wanted. But that was okay. Teo and I may not have spoken as long as I had wanted, but the intense eye contact we sustained during the whole conversation made up for it. After Ira ordered, Morgan turned to me and J.D. "Anybody want to split some onion rings?"

She had no takers. "Just order them," I told her. "This is on me, remember?"

"I don't want the whole thing." She turned to the waitress. "I'll just have a chocolate milkshake."

"You know what," Ira butted in. "Can I change my order? Half fries, half onion rings."

"You hate onion rings," Morgan reminded him.

"But you don't," he said, his hazel eyes lighting up as he looked at her.

Even though they had been going out for an eternity, Ira still managed to make Morgan blush. I saw her take his hand under the table and squeeze it.

J.D. leaned over to me. "Are they always like that?"

"Always."

He didn't say anything else, but I'm sure he thought they were incredibly cheesy. I didn't, though. I thought they were sickeningly sweet. I wanted someone who looked at me like that.

"Hey, T," some guy on the team who I didn't recognize called out to Teo. "Look at this. Someone beat your score."

"No they didn't," he said, standing up and heading toward his friend.

I looked to J.D. for an explanation.

"You never play the games here?" he asked.

"Nope."

"Well, your boyfriend does," he said.

"Shh," I warned him.

"What? No one's listening. They're all ready to watch Teo reclaim his top spot."

In the corner of the diner was an old Ms. Pac-Man machine. A large group was now surrounding it.

"I told you," J.D. said, nodding toward Teo, "he loves the eighties."

"I thought you meant music."

"No, I meant all of it."

Okay, there were worse things in the world. So what if he had a slight obsession with the eighties? He was smart and handsome and kind and successful. The rest didn't matter.

"He's hooked on that game," J.D. continued. "He's had the top score forever. Whenever we go out, he always picks this place so he can make sure he's still winning." He looked over at his cousin. "Get him some sort of eighties game for one of his gifts, and he'll love you forever."

I liked the sound of that.

There was a slew of people around Teo, watching him play. I decided I needed to get in on that, so I got up and squeezed through the crowd until I was next to him.

"Come on, come on," he said to the machine as he chased after a bunch of blue ghosts on the screen. He was doing really well. He made it past six levels and hadn't lost any lives yet.

"Go, go, go," he said as the ghosts changed colors. One of them almost caught up to him, but he managed to get away.

He was intense as he made it to the next level. His concentration was almost the same as on the football field. He maneuvered Ms. Pac-Man around the maze. It was actually kind of mesmerizing. I saw how you could get hooked. He made it three more levels until a pink ghost changed directions and headed straight for him.

As ridiculous as it sounds, I actually gasped.

Teo couldn't get away fast enough. The ghost caught up to him, and he lost a life. "Damn it," he said and hit the machine.

It was loud enough to make me flinch.

"It's okay," I said, "you'll get it this time."

"Yeah," he mumbled and started playing again.

"You can do it," I said, and then applauded.

Only it was like I was invisible. He didn't even acknowledge my presence, not when I cheered, not in between lives or rounds, and not even when I asked a simple question like "What's the top level you've gotten to?"

Don't take it personally, don't take it personally, I told myself. Teo was in the zone. He wanted to win; I couldn't fault him for that. If that were me, I'd be just as focused. I wouldn't want somebody interrupting me and breaking my concentration.

Still . . . if it was a guy I liked, and it was just a silly game at a diner . . .

I let myself fall back into the crowd and eventually went back to the table.

"What was that?" Morgan asked. I had hoped she hadn't seen that. While she backed my plan a hundred percent, she still wasn't totally on the Teo bandwagon. "He was totally rud—"

I held up my hand for her to stop. I didn't want to hear it. "He just likes to win."

"He's—" J.D. started, but I cut him off, too.

"Let's drop it, okay?" I asked. "He was just in the zone."

The waitress brought over my grilled cheese just in time, and I distracted myself with my sandwich.

"Teo," J.D. called to him. "Your food's here."

A few minutes later Teo came back over and was in much better spirits. "Champion twice today," he said.

I couldn't bring myself to look up. "Congratulations," I told him.

"Thanks," he said, sounding completely upbeat.

Maybe I had been overreacting. It hadn't been about me. He just wanted to come in first. If anyone understood that, it was yours truly.

J.D. got up to take some pictures, and I just sat there. I was trying to be positive, but that moment Teo and I shared earlier seemed so far away. He was so focused on his teammates that I was beginning to feel like he didn't even see me. Morgan tried making small talk, but I wasn't in the mood. I just wanted everyone to finish eating so I could leave without calling attention to myself.

J.D. returned to his chair and put a poinsettia in front of me. "Look at this. Your favorite."

I tossed the french fry I was holding back on my plate. "Hardly."

"What do you have against poinsettias?" Teo asked, all of his attention suddenly focused back on me.

I saw J.D. opening his mouth, so I beat him to the punch. "They kill cats, and I'm a huge cat lover, that's all."

"That's not true," J.D. said, snapping my picture.

If he told everyone my mall story, he was a dead man.

"*Yeah*, it is."

"*Actually*," J.D. said, giving me that irritating smile of his, "that's a myth. Poinsettias may make cats sick, but they probably won't kill them. They get a bad rap for nothing."

Not that I loved being corrected in public, but at least he didn't share the mortification of me sitting on the floor as a bunch of dirt and pots rained down on my head. "Fine, maybe I just think they're overexposed. There are a lot of beautiful red flowers. Why not a Gerbera daisy? Why does the poinsettia get Christmas?"

"Well," J.D. answered, "because some say the shape symbolizes the Star of Bethlehem."

"I was asking *rhetorically*."

"Ignore him," Teo said, coming to my rescue. "He just likes to pretend he's the smart one in the family."

J.D. shrugged. "If the shoe fits . . ."

Teo laughed. "Uh-huh. Want to compare grades?"

But Teo didn't have to prove anything to me. I knew how smart he was; I had done my research. Top in his class, AP courses, and, if the rumors were true, an SAT score that had me salivating.

Reggie threw some money on the table and whispered something to Teo. I tried to make it out. It sounded like a few of them were going back to his house, but I clearly wasn't on the short list.

"Okay, ride leaves now," Reggie said.

Teo stood up, dropped some cash, and gave me a quick smile. "Sorry, I've—"

"Gotta go," Reggie finished for him and basically ushered him out. About ten others left with him. When Teo got to the door, he looked over in my direction and shrugged in what seemed like an it's-not-my-fault-don't-blame-me kind of way. I tried to smile back, but I wasn't really feeling it. Pretty soon the table was practically empty. Almost everyone else had filed out, too.

"How did we wind up in charge of the bill?" Morgan asked as she counted the money that had been left behind.

"I guess they know you're good at math," I told her.

"Yeah, I'm sure that's it." She handed the money to Ira and asked him and J.D. to bring it to the register.

I didn't like where this was headed. "I know what you're thinking," I said. "He didn't say a proper good-bye, he just left me here. It wasn't intentional. His friends swarmed him, it's a big night for them, Teo just got caught up."

"Charlie, I saw your face all night. After you came back from the Ms. Pac-Man game, you looked miserable."

"Teo didn't do anything I wouldn't do."

She crossed her arms. "You are not like that."

"Yes I am. Do you not remember when I spelled *ptyalagogue* wrong at the spelling bee? I stormed off the stage, and I was so angry I was shaking."

She clutched the table. "That was five years ago, so: a) you really need to let that go; b) you are incredible, and there are a ton of guys who'd want to go to Noelle's party with you; and c) a guy you are thinking about dating should make you feel special—not like you're a distraction or something he can ignore."

"He doesn't," I objected. "He's just had a crazy day. You'll see. Once he gets to know me, everything will be perfect."

"And if it's not?"

I turned away from her, tears threatening to fill my eyes. "It has to be. You know what happened with Zakiyah. Besides, Teo is a great guy. Have you forgotten the volunteering thing? Just please cut him—and me—some slack. You'll see he's worth it. Please?"

"Okay, sorry," she said, taking a deep breath. "I don't want to fight. Come over Monday. We can work on the paper, and then I'll make the cookies for Teo. I'll help you however you need."

I knew she was talking about a lot more than Operation Secret Santa.

"Thanks," I said as J.D. and Ira came back over to us.

"Ready?" Ira asked.

Was I ever.

Ira held up a cupcake in a little box. "Guess what I bought?"

"Why?" Morgan asked. "I can give you a million of those for free."

He shrugged. "I want to support you. If they see they're selling, they'll order more."

She wrapped her arms around him, and they walked outside.

J.D. and I followed. "Need a ride?" I asked him. He went out of his way for me today; it was the least I could do for him.

"Ira offered since I'm right next to Morgan." He studied my face. "Are you okay?"

"Yeah. Just thinking about my next step in Operation Secret Santa."

"Is that what we're calling it now?" he asked.

"We are." But the truth was, I was thinking about what Morgan had said. I watched as she and Ira walked ahead, arm in arm, talking and laughing. I wanted a guy like that—one who was there for me, who made me laugh until it hurt, who came out to dinner even though he'd already eaten just so he could spend time with me, who ordered onion rings just because I liked them, who bought a cupcake he didn't need, because I made it.

Morgan didn't seem to think that person could be Teo, but I did.

Now more than ever, I hoped I was right.

Seventeen

N o way, no way, no way, no way, no way," I said as I got to my locker Monday morning.

Taped to the door was a red Gerbera daisy. I ripped open the note that was attached. It said: *Thought you deserved the "new" Christmas flower.*

Where was Morgan? She usually met me by now, and I needed her because there was a decent chance I was going to pass out. This flower had to have come from Teo. The only people at the diner who were part of the Secret Santa were Morgan, J.D., Roger, and Teo. And Morgan and J.D. already told me whose names they picked, Roger was sitting at one of the outside booths nowhere near me, so that just left Teo!

I knew I was right about him. He *was* a sweet, good guy. He was just crazed and in a football-winning high at the diner. And he was making up for it now.

I closed my eyes and took a long whiff of the flower.

"Look at you," Morgan said. "It's just what you wanted."

And then it hit me. The Gerbera daisy wasn't from Teo. It was from my best friend, who was picking up the slack for my Secret Santa. "You did this, didn't you?"

"Wasn't me," she said, but she was all smiles, and I couldn't tell if she was lying.

"You look guilty," I told her.

"I'm just happy you got something nice."

I looked from the flower to her. "And you had nothing to do with this? Ira, either?"

"Nope."

I needed to be sure. "And neither of you told someone else to do this or what to get me?"

"Charlie, why are you acting like a bad TV show detective? Someone got you a gift; it's a good thing!"

I lightly pulled at one of the petals. "I know, I just want to make sure this wasn't you, because that means it was probably Teo!"

I explained my process of elimination, but she wasn't nearly as excited as I was about the whole thing.

"That means he also gave you the crushed candy cane that you thought was pretty much the worst gift ever," she pointed out.

"True," I said, taking another sniff of the flower. "But that was also before last night. I'm telling you, we had a moment before he got all distracted. And now I know for sure that he felt it, too. See, he came through. You said I deserved someone who made me feel special, and he did. He showed he listened and went out of his way for me. You have to admit this is a great start. It makes up for Friday night."

"All right," she said, and linked arms with me. "In the holiday spirit, I will give Teo the benefit of the doubt and a second chance. You like him, so I like him."

"Good," I said as we headed to homeroom.

I kept the flower sticking out of my bag all day so I could sneak peeks at it. Every time I did, I couldn't help but smile.

J.D. took the seat next to me in study hall and tossed his bag next to mine. "Careful," I snapped. "Don't crush my flower."

"Sorry." He pulled it from my bag. "Since when did you start carrying foliage around with you?"

I grabbed it back. "Since my Secret Santa got it for me. It's from Teo."

J.D. didn't look surprised, he just nodded, which confirmed my suspicions a hundred percent. Of course Teo would tell his cousin whose name he drew from the jar. It also explained why J.D. got weird when I told him about the broken candy cane. He knew who it was from. But it didn't matter now; Teo was bringing his A game.

"Why are you sitting here anyway?" I asked.

Normally J.D. sat on the opposite side of the room.

"I can leave," he said, and picked up his bag. "But then we have to spend our free time plotting 'Operation Secret Santa.'" He made air quotes around the name. "Although we both know this is just an elaborate scheme so you can hang around with me more."

I took his bag from him and put it back on the ground. I

definitely didn't want to have to deal with any more outside-of-school time alone with J.D. "Yes, you caught me. Why would I want Teo, when I can have his never-on-time, likes-to-push-my-buttons, irritating cousin? Don't think I didn't notice you were late for the last *Sentinel* meeting."

"I was busy," he said.

"But you have a commitment. And now you have even more responsibility. You're in charge of all the photos in . . ." I stopped myself. I didn't need to get into it with J.D. Not today. My day was going too well to ruin it by fighting with him. Instead, I changed the subject. "I took your suggestion. I went online and found a Donkey Kong Jr. key chain. You can actually play the game on it. It should arrive any day now."

"Nice," he said.

I was pretty impressed with myself. I did a lot of Google searching to find the key chain at a cheap price. It wasn't Ms. Pac-Man (that one cost a fortune), but Donkey Kong was another eighties hit. I was confident that Teo would like it. With that and the cookies, I was good on the gift front. My problem was face time. I didn't want to wait until the *Sentinel*'s holiday party to get some quality one-on-one conversations going. If I wanted him to take me to Noelle's party, I needed to set that in motion much earlier. Fortunately, my ticket in had just taken a seat next to me. "Now I have to figure out how to get more Teo time."

"Are you sure this is what you want?"

Was I sure? What kind of question was that? "Obviously."

"You know he dates around a lot, right?" J.D. asked.

"Probably because he hasn't found the right person. Me,"

I said, pointing to myself. "But he'll never know that if I don't get to spend more time with him. I need to think of something special. Maybe something Christmasy. It's supposed to be magical, right?"

"You could come over to my house tomorrow," he said.

"Let me clarify. Something Christmasy with Teo, not with you."

"No kidding," he said. "But have you forgotten he's my cousin? My family got our tree last night, and we're decorating it then. Teo and his little brother, Dylan, are stopping by. That kid would decorate every tree in Sandbrook if you let him."

I couldn't blame him; I would, too. Only I wasn't a little kid, so while the idea of decorating a tree with Teo gave me goose bumps, I couldn't intrude like that. I shook my head. "Thank you, it actually sounds really nice, but I couldn't . . ."

It was sweet that their whole family was doing it together. I was a little jealous, even though I knew I shouldn't be. I got to decorate a tree with my mom. Sure, it was the shortcut version of what we usually did, but we were still together. That's what mattered. Still, I missed our traditions.

"Earth to Charlie," J.D. said, pulling me from my thoughts.

"What?" I asked.

"You should come join us."

I bit my lip. "Really?"

"Yeah."

I couldn't tell if he was just trying to keep his part of the deal to get me time with Teo or if he sensed how down in the dumps I was about the holidays and was trying to do his good deed for the year by inviting me. But I didn't want to be the weirdo popping by a classmate's tree decorating. Especially when we weren't even friends. "Won't your family think it's strange if I show up?"

"No, are you kidding? My mom will go crazy over having more people there. My parents aren't picking up my sister from school until this weekend. My mom will love having a full house to help decorate. She keeps saying how it feels too empty."

"But if it's just me, won't your parents *and* Teo get the wrong idea about us?"

"You mean you and me?" J.D. leaned back in his chair. "Worried they'll wonder how you landed such a ravishingly handsome boyfriend with such a sharp sense of humor and artistic prowess?"

I gave him the stank eye.

"Fine," he said, laughing, his dimple looking bigger than ever. "Invite Morgan and Ira, or someone else. Seriously, my parents won't care."

"And Teo's definitely going to be there?"

"Definitely."

This day had gone from great to spectacular. Not only was I going to get to decorate a real Christmas tree, but I was going to get to do it with Teo.

I looked at J.D. and smiled. "Count me in."

Eighteen

Morgan shut her laptop. "I think that should do it. All the articles have been through copyediting, Zakiyah's gossip letter contained nothing about you—"

"Because she knew I'd cut it," I said.

Morgan ignored me and continued her list. "We did our editorial letter, the layout has been reset to include Teo's article and the photo spread, now we just need J.D. to turn it in and this issue is in the can."

"In other words," I said, "we are a long way from done." The last person we could count on to hand things in on time was J.D.

Morgan gathered up her stuff from her kitchen table and cleared off all the mock-ups we had printed. "We told him he has until next Wednesday night. As long as it's in then, we can run everything Thursday and hand them out Friday."

"Sounds to me like we're cutting it awfully close." I looked at my schedule and put a question mark near "finish holiday edition of *Sentinel*." Unfortunately, it was no longer in my hands.

"Don't worry, it will still fit your timeline." She pointed to the paper in front of me. "Checking off who's been naughty or nice?"

"Don't make fun, this keeps me sane."

"Believe me, I know," she said.

Everyone who knew me did. I lived and breathed by my schedule, and I had a lot to do between now and Christmas. It was exactly two weeks away, and being organized was the only way to make sure I got it all done.

I looked over my list of things to do again. I had finished my English essay, was caught up on my studies for midterms, orders and invoices were up to date for our bakery business, so I was on track. The only thing I was falling behind on was getting Teo to ask me out. I needed to step up my game.

I placed my schedule back in my bag. "I should get going. My mom is actually home tonight, and we're going to decorate a gingerbread house."

Morgan raised her eyebrow at me.

"Yeah, don't worry. We bought it premade." Morgan knew my mom was about as talented in the kitchen as I was—and she saw the disaster we baked last year. "We're just putting on tons of icing, gumdrops, licorice, and M&M's, basically making a gooey candy mess."

"I want pictures."

"You got it," I told her.

"Don't forget these." She handed me a container of Jim Dandies as I walked to the door. "Teo is going to love them. They're delicious, if I do say so myself."

If Morgan made them, I knew they were. "Thank you." She really was the best.

I was pretty excited as I drove back to my place. Things were looking up. I was going to decorate a Christmas tree with Teo the next day, I had his favorite cookies to surprise him with, and my mom and I were finally going to do one of our yearly Christmas traditions the right way.

My mother's car was in the driveway when I got home. *Yes! She made it back on time.*

I rushed in the house. I couldn't help but smile when I saw all the decorating supplies were already on the dining room table. This was really happening! I couldn't wait. If last year was any indication, we were going to create the ugliest (but most delicious) gingerbread house in the world. There would be enough sugary snacks on it to give the tooth fairy nightmares and satiate my sweet tooth until next December. "Mom," I called out.

There was no answer.

"Mom?"

She wasn't in the dining room or kitchen. I poked my head in the living room and let out a sigh. She was on the couch. Fast asleep.

Part of me wanted to wake her up, but I couldn't bring myself to do it. I knew how little sleep she'd been going on, and she looked so peaceful. I took the afghan off the recliner and covered her.

It caused her to stir. "Charlie?" she said, sitting up.

"Go back to sleep, it's okay."

"No, no, I was just closing my eyes for a second. I'm fine. I'm up." Her words didn't match her demeanor. She looked like she was going to conk out again. "We have a gingerbread house to decorate."

I knew she wanted to spend the time with me, and vice versa, but not this way. How much fun was it going to be if she had to fight to keep her eyes open? "We can do it another time."

"Come here." She patted the seat next to her, and I went over, trying not to show my disappointment.

She put her arm around me. "I know this has been tough for you. It's been tough for me, too. The new job has a learning curve, and not only am I doing everything this job entails, I'm handling all of my old workload, too. They have someone new starting after the first of the year, and things should settle down then. I know that doesn't make it better now, but there is a light at the end of the tunnel."

I nodded.

She pulled me closer and kissed the top of my head. "I love you, sweetie, and I know this is your favorite time of year, and . . ." Her voice choked up. "And I'm so sorry that I'm ruining it for you. That's the last thing I wanted."

Seeing her about to cry was making me tear up. "You're not ruining it." I wiped the corner of my eye.

"You know you're the most important thing to me, right?"

"I know."

"Good," she said. "Now, let's go decorate a gingerbread house."

"You need your sleep. It's not a big deal. You don't have to," I told her.

"But I want to." She stood up. "Let's go." Then she took my hands and pulled me to my feet and into a big bear hug. "I love you, sweetie."

I squeezed her back. "I love you, too."

"We don't have a lot of time this Christmas, but we can make the most of what we have." She led me to the dining room. "Now let's see if we can top last year's creation."

And as we piled on one piece of candy after another, I got a slight taste of what I'd been missing all season, and it was just what I wanted.

The only problem was—I craved more.

Nineteen

I dropped off the cookies for Teo in his homeroom, but I wasn't sure if he tried them or even got them. I waited for him after history, but he didn't walk in my direction. The same thing happened yesterday, and ever since football ended, he seemed to be bolting out of school at the end of the day. He was probably volunteering more now, which was great, but that made it harder to catch him. Other than a quick glance and wave on my way to English yesterday, I hadn't seen him at all, and I was getting antsy. We hadn't spoken since the diner. Sure, he gave me the flower, but I needed face time.

It made the tree decorating at J.D.'s even more crucial.

He called it for 6:30, and I, of course, was right on time, yet I didn't go in. I parked in front of Morgan's and just sat there watching the minutes on my phone pass by. 6:31. 6:32. 6:33. It killed me not to get out of the car and go ring the doorbell. I hated being late; the idea alone made me feel a little nauseous, and intentionally doing it was ten times worse. But Teo hadn't shown up yet. Neither had Morgan and Ira. They weren't getting there until closer to 7:30. It was the first night of Hanukkah, and they were lighting candles and opening presents with their families first. The idea of being alone with just J.D. and his parents seemed weird. Yet when the time read 6:35, I couldn't take it anymore. I had to go in. Being late was rude, and I made such a big deal about the importance of punctuality with J.D. that I had no choice.

I braced myself as I rang the doorbell. I could do this. I'd been through worse.

J.D. opened the door, and if he noticed I was late, he didn't say anything. "Hey, come in." "A Holly Jolly Christmas" was playing over a little speaker on the mantel, and a fire was burning in the fireplace. It had a really nice feel. J.D. pointed to the couple trying to unknot a strand of lights. "Those are my parents."

"Hi," I said.

"Hi," Mr. Ortiz answered back.

"You must be Charlie," Mrs. Ortiz said, dropping the lights and coming over to greet me. "We're glad you could come. J.D. has told us a lot about you."

His cheeks turned a light shade of pink. "All bad, I assure you," he said.

Mrs. Ortiz gave him a loving squeeze on his shoulder and then shifted her focus back to me. "We hear you're the coeditor of the paper and top of your class. Sounds very impressive."

"Thank you," I said.

"And are you—"

A timer went off in the kitchen.

Mrs. Ortiz turned to her husband. "Honey, will you go check on that?"

"Why don't we both go," he answered, "and give the kids some time alone."

Time *alone*? I certainly hoped his parents didn't think this was a date or that J.D. and I were into each other. He was *not* the guy I wanted to be linked to.

While I was worrying that the Ortizes—and ultimately Teo—would get the wrong idea, J.D. actually looked relieved his dad was steering his mom away from me. Mr. Ortiz handed J.D. the Christmas lights. "Why don't you and Charlie work on these?"

Ugh. I needed to amend my statement about loving to decorate Christmas trees. I loved the actual decorating part, but the dealing with knotted wire—not so much. But I wasn't going to say anything.

"Sorry," he said, giving me one end of the lights, "my mom loves meeting my friends." Friends? Well, I was over at his house. I guess his mom wouldn't assume that her son and I couldn't stand each other a good chunk of the time.

"She's really nice," I said.

"Yeah. Well, I hope you are prepared to eat," J.D. continued. "Both my parents like to feed people when they come over, and I think they may be going a little overboard."

"Morgan and her family are the same way. My mom and I are more takeout experts."

For the next five minutes, J.D. and I attempted to detangle

the lights in silence. Then we were forced to work together. "I think your end needs to go through mine. Here," he said, showing me a big loop. "Walk through this."

"That will just twist it in another direction," I protested.

"Just try it."

"Fine."

I did and guess what? I was right. "See?"

"No, we're okay. I just need to go this way." He moved around me to the left and pulled the strand of lights through another loop. "And now you need to go that way."

"That makes no sense," I said. "I'd be better off going the other direction and putting my end through there." Before I knew it, he was going one way and I was going the other, and we were tangled up like in a bad game of Twister, only standing and wrapped in lights.

I was so close to J.D., I could smell him. A combination of shampoo, dryer sheets, Christmas tree, and boy. I cursed myself for taking a second whiff. *Why would I try and smell J.D.? What is wrong with me?*

"Get us out of here," I said, and he circled one more time, only instead of freeing me from this mess, he brought me face-to-face with him. Well, my face to his chest. He was a head taller than I am.

If I didn't know better, I would have thought he did it on purpose.

I put my hands up to push him away. *Oh.* His abs were a lot harder than I imagined. *Stop it, Charlie. Move your hands off him. Eww. Why would you linger?* The Christmas music was clearly affecting my brain. I tilted my head up, and our eyes latched. I quickly looked away and took a step back, as I made myself shove him away.

He spun back in the other direction, and I could feel myself letting out a sigh of relief.

"Okay," he said, lifting some lights over his head and freeing himself, "maybe your way was right."

Just then there was a light knock at the door, and Teo and his brother walked in.

J.D.'s parents heard them and came out. "If it isn't my favorite nephews," Mrs. Ortiz said and gave them both a big hug. J.D. went over and clasped hands with Teo and then turned to his brother, who couldn't have been more than six. "Dylaaan," J.D. called out, and he picked up the little boy and spun him through the air as he laughed.

Teo came over to me. He looked so good. He was wearing a dark-red sweater. It was definitely his color. Although any color would have been amazing on him. I tried to keep my breathing in check. *Don't get flustered.* But of course he had to walk in while I was draped in Christmas lights. "Looks like you could use some help."

"Maybe a little," I admitted.

He unwrapped the wire from around me and within a couple of minutes had the whole thing unknotted. It figured. The guy I didn't want, I wound up tied to, while the one I would have loved to be roped together with had no issues untangling the lights. Although, I couldn't say I was surprised. Teo was at the top of the class at everything.

"Thanks," I said.

"We have a ton of food to snack on," Mr. Ortiz said. "We'll bring it out here, and then we can get started on the tree. Sound like a plan?"

We all nodded.

"And, Teo, I have your favorite for dessert," Mrs. Ortiz said and then turned toward Dylan. "Want to come help your uncle and me bring out dinner?"

Once they left, Teo slapped J.D. on the back. "The eighties music was a pretty big giveaway, but Aunt Jackie's cookies this morning? I knew you were my Secret Santa. Those cookies were seriously good."

Crap, crap, crap, crap, crap.

I should have known this would happen. Of course Teo would think that J.D. was giving him the gifts. Who else would know that much about him?

"Shh," J.D. warned him. "Don't let my mom hear you calling those your favorite. She didn't make Aunt Jackie's cookies. She made buñuelos."

"Okay, I like those, too. So you made the Jim Dandies yourself? Impressive."

"No, I'm not your Secret Santa."

"Right, because everyone knows the cookie my aunt used to make when I was a kid?" Teo asked.

What was I supposed to do? Admit it was me? I wanted Teo to get to know me better *before* he realized I was the one who got him all these specially thought out gifts. Okay. I needed to calm down. Maybe it wasn't so bad if he knew. Maybe it would even make him like me more. He was sweet with the flower; this was just me doing the same thing back. Besides, he was going to find out the truth eventually anyway. But what if it backfired? No. I just had to steer him away from J.D.

"Your cousin's telling the truth," I confided in him. I lowered my voice and tried to be flirty. "Don't tell, but he has Katie. My guess," I said, giving him a big smile, "someone asked J.D. for help so they get the Secret Santa thing right. You *deserve* good gifts," I said, making sure to use the word Teo wrote to me.

I saw J.D. roll his eyes, but his cousin wasn't facing him, so I didn't care.

"Yeah?" Teo asked and moved closer to me, his eyes locked on mine. "You think so?"

"I think just about everyone on the paper does," I said, trying to keep my Secret Santa cover. "It's what I would have done if I'd drawn your name."

"If . . . ," he repeated. "So I guess that means you didn't get me?"

"Unfortunately, I can neither confirm nor deny that. I already broke the Secret Santa code once by telling you about Katie, and I can't afford a rep as an editor who divulges sources or off-the-record information. We wouldn't want that now, would we?"

"No, we wouldn't," he said, still looking at me in a way that made my cheeks warm. I wasn't sure what was going on, but I liked it.

The moment didn't last long. His brother burst into the room.

"Look at all of this," Dylan said, carrying a large tray filled with chicken, beef, and vegetable skewers. We all turned to face him.

"Finally," J.D. mumbled.

"Let me help you with that, bud," Teo said and took the platter from him and placed it on the coffee table. Then he ruffled Dylan's hair.

If I liked Teo before, watching him with his brother tripled it. The two of them were sweet together. I liked seeing this side of Teo.

"Dig in," Mr. Ortiz said, carrying out another tray. His had a whole selection of hors d'oeuvres. There were six different ones to choose from.

"Wow, you made all of this? Thank you, this is really impressive," I said.

"The hors d'oeuvres are from a box," J.D. whispered, but loud enough for his mother to hear.

She laughed and threw a napkin at him. "Don't give away our secrets. But he's right. Everything else is homemade, though."

After we all finished stuffing our faces, Mrs. Ortiz opened up the boxes filled with the Christmas decorations. "Shall we?" she asked, and we all moved over to the tree.

"I want to do the tinsel," Dylan said.

I handed it to him, and he threw some on the lower branches.

J.D. picked him up. "We need some up here." Then he said, "But we can't forget the other side, right? Ready, Teo?" Then he literally threw Dylan to him. I thought my heart was going to fall to my toes. Teo caught him with no problem, and it was only two feet, but still!

Then Teo said, "I don't know, J.D. What do you think? Your side may need a little more, huh?"

"I think so," he answered.

Then Teo threw Dylan back.

Please don't drop him.

J.D. made the catch, and I seemed to be the only one in the group having a slight panic attack. Dylan was loving it, and all of the Ortizes were laughing. Maybe this was what it was like growing up with a big family. Or just boys. I was an only child, and I didn't have any cousins. I wasn't exactly used to big family affairs, other than the ones I crashed at Morgan's. And she certainly wasn't flinging her cousins or brother through the air.

I will admit that by the end, the little's boy laughter was pretty contagious and it was cute to see Teo and J.D. making him such a big part of the night. But I was still relieved when they put him down and started hanging up the ornaments.

"Any special order?" I asked.

"Anywhere's fine," Mrs. Ortiz said.

"Let me guess," J.D. said, hanging up a heart-shaped photo ornament of his parents. "You have a detailed chart of where every decoration on your tree must go, including the exact distance specifications."

"Not true at all." That was only a half lie. I didn't care which decorations were used because they were mostly the same. The past few years, I preferred the elegant look. So my mom and I went with little white lights, glass icicles, and cream and gold ornaments and ribbons. But generally, I was particular about the spacing. You couldn't have too many things clustered in one spot or have an empty patch. It needed to be just right. But since Mom and I had worked at warp speed, this year's tree didn't have the usual showroom quality. I'd thought about fixing it on my own the next day, but it felt wrong to do it without her, so I'd left it. Now it was just a reminder of how imperfect this month had been.

Instead of explaining, I decided to ignore J.D. and concentrate on decorating instead. I pulled out an ornament. It was a bronzed baby shoe.

"Look," Mrs. Ortiz said to her husband, "J.D.'s first little shoe." She started to get misty eyed.

"Way to not embarrass me, Mom," he said.

"Don't worry, I'll cry over your sister's shoe, too."

"Wait until she gets to the handprints," Teo said.

"Or the papier-mâché ornaments, or the picture ones, or just about any of them," J.D. added.

"Don't make fun of your mother," she said, and wiped her eyes, but you could tell how happy she was.

"We made all of the ornaments," J.D. said, and as I looked through the box, I could see he was telling the truth. Even the regular ball ornaments had been hand painted. "Every year we each make a new one to add to the tree."

"I made some, too!" Dylan said, and pointed to the first ornament he put up—a Spider-Man Shrinky Dink.

"Very cool," I told him. And I meant it. As I looked at their tree coming to life, I was a bit in awe. It told the story of their family.

This was the Christmas I wanted. Only with my mom. I tried to push away the hollow feeling in my gut as they pulled out ornament after ornament and shared stories and memories about aunts, uncles, cousins, grandparents, and more. I loved how close they were and how each decoration seemed to have a life of its own. It also made me a little sad. But maybe next year I'd have this, too.

As we neared the end of the final box, I reached in and pulled out the last ornament.

"Um?" I said. It was a decapitated Barbie doll head with an ornament hook going through her forehead. That, I could live without.

J.D. took it from me and laughed. "Leeza."

"Huh?" I asked.

"My sister," J.D. explained, carefully placing it on the tree, and not on the side hidden by the wall, either. "About ten years ago she was being a real b—"

"*Difficult pre-teen,*" Mrs. Ortiz interrupted.

"Yes," J.D. continued, "a difficult pre-teen and didn't want to make an ornament. She got so annoyed about my parents talking about tradition that she went in her closet, pulled out an old doll, jammed the ornament hook in its face, and said, 'Here! Happy?' And my parents said yes and put it up on the tree. By Christmas Leeza felt bad and tried to take it down, but they insisted it stay. It was a little tense at the time, but now it's a running joke, and Barbie's head has a permanent place of honor on our tree. We all laugh when we look at it."

"We're almost finished," Mr. Ortiz said. "Just one more thing."

He went to the mantel above the fireplace and reached into a small box. He pulled out an exquisite Star of Bethlehem.

"Our grandfather made that," Teo told me. "I have one just like it on my tree at home."

"He *made* that?" I asked.

"Yeah, he's pretty talented. He had a workshop where he played around with a lot of things. Painting, metal, glass, wood, electronics. He's kind of amazing."

"I can tell." The star was made of glass, had gold trim, and had intricate detailing carved throughout. It must have taken him weeks to do.

"I wish he could be here with us this year, but he doesn't want to do the winter," Mr. Ortiz said, and I saw J.D. bite his lip.

"It's our first Christmas with him in Florida," Teo said, slapping J.D. on the back. "He moved closer to my aunt Jackie. Said he was too old for snow."

I could tell how much he meant to both of them.

"How about dessert?" J.D. said, changing the subject.

"Yes!" Dylan answered for all of us.

Morgan and Ira got there just in time to join us. "Sorry we're late," she said, and handed Mrs. Ortiz a box with bow tied around it. "Merry Christmas."

Of course Morgan brought something. Why hadn't I thought of that?

Mrs. Ortiz read the card and then untied the ribbon and peeked inside. "Morgan, Ira, Charlie, thank you all. I love peppermint bark. Especially the homemade kind."

Why was she thanking me? I didn't do anything. I looked over at Morgan, and she winked at me. She must have signed my name to the card, too.

Thank you, I mouthed to her. "Oh, I almost forgot. Happy Hanukkah! Did you guys have fun?"

"Yeah," Morgan said, "it was really great. But I ate so much, I am stuffed."

"Well, I hope you have room for a little more," Mr. Ortiz said. "We have Christmas cookies and buñuelos."

"What is that?" Morgan asked.

"It's like a fried dough ball. We cover it in powdered sugar." That sounded like my kind of dessert. Morgan's, too.

"I think I can make some room," she said.

"Great," Mr. Ortiz said. "And how about hot chocolate?" The Ortizes really were wonderful hosts, and they definitely knew how to create that Christmas feeling.

"I can never say no to that," Morgan said.

"Any other takers?" Mr. Ortiz asked.

Everyone said yes except me.

"Wait, you don't like hot chocolate?" J.D. asked. "First poinsettias, now this?"

"I prefer to eat my chocolate, not drink it," I answered. "But I like the little marshmallows."

"Next thing you're going to tell us is that you don't like Santa or sleigh bells or mistletoe."

I did not want to talk about mistletoe with him. Teo, on the other hand, was a whole other story.

"I like all Christmas traditions," I said, avoiding specifics.

"Does that mean you're joining the boys to go caroling on Thursday?" Mrs. Ortiz asked.

I turned to J.D. and Teo. "Wait, you guys go caroling?" I so wanted in on this.

"There's nothing wrong with caroling," Teo said, grabbing

a piece of Morgan's peppermint bark, his posture tensing. "Besides, I like to sing."

"I didn't say there was anything wrong with it." I hoped I hadn't offended him. "I just didn't picture you guys out there."

"J.D., me, and a bunch of people from my church are going."

"Don't misunderstand," I said. "I think it's awesome. I'm just jealous. I've always wanted to do that."

"Yeah?" he said, loosening back up.

"Yeah."

"Then you should come." He gave me one of his killer smiles, and I couldn't help but return it with one of my own.

"I think I will."

"Good."

Mr. Ortiz brought out a tray filled with mugs of hot chocolate. Teo took a marshmallow off the top of his and handed it to me.

It might not have been much, just a small gesture, but it was from Teo. To me. And it was absolutely perfect.

Twenty

My Christmas was looking up, and so were my chances of going to Noelle's with Teo. Sure it was just a little flirting, but it was definitely a step in the right direction. I couldn't stop thinking about it, not even a couple of days later. I was still practically floating on Thursday, and then I walked into history class. And my whole WEEK got better. Mr. Magocsi handed me a little box. "Someone left this for you," he said.

For *me*? Here? It had to be Teo. I was getting those excited, nervous chills, not so different from the ones on Christmas morning, but maybe a little better since this gift was from a boy and not my mom. I took my seat, pulled the red ribbon off, and looked inside. I couldn't help but let out an *awww!* Teo gave me marshmallows, but not just any marshmallows. They were in the shape of kittens. There were not too many things that made me giddy (besides maybe Teo and winning a competition), but kittens always turned me to mush. And little marshmallow ones that came from the boy I'd been dreaming about? Come on! The adorable factor was off the charts. How was it possible that I wasn't already a puddle on the ground?

J.D. walked into class and took his seat. He was diagonally behind me. "What are you smiling about?"

I was so happy, I didn't even give some snarky response. And I guess—credit where credit was due—J.D. did help make this a reality. I held up the box. "This. And your cousin. I mean, I thought what happened at your house was great, but this . . ."

"What happened at my house?" he asked, leaning forward in his chair.

"We had a moment. A *really* good moment. And now there's this." I pulled the box closer. I hadn't even noticed there was a tiny card tucked inside.

I tore it out of the envelope. *Maybe this will make you like hot chocolate a little better. They're almost as cute as you.*

I put the card down and just stared at it. How was this real? Teo Ortiz went so above and beyond. He not only remembered me talking about marshmallows, but he also remembered I mentioned that I liked cats at the diner. Then he went out and got me the perfect gift. "I swear, he is the sweetest, nicest, most adorable guy ever."

J.D. pulled out a pen and a notebook. "Are we still talking about Teo?"

"Very funny."

"Hey," he said, drawing something on one of the blank pages. "I love the guy. But *adorable*? Come on. Besides, I would bet he prefers hot. And *sweet*? I'd go with smooth. Or maybe charismatic. Or player-ish."

I shot him a glare. "Don't do that. He's not. Or maybe he was before, what do I know, but this is different. Players don't go out of their way like this. They don't have to."

"Don't you think you and Teo are maybe a little *different*?" he asked.

I let out a little snort. Why did he have to try to bring me down? "Because he's popular and I'm not? Who cares? We're both smart, we're both at the top of our classes, we both have more awards and trophies than we know what to do with. Maybe he wants someone who can keep up with him."

"I'm just trying to say that he's just . . . um."

I could feel my face getting hot. "Better-looking? Is that what you're getting at?"

"No, you're—"

"Just stop. I don't care what you think about my appearance. I look fine, and"—I waved the card in my hand—"apparently Teo thinks so, too."

"Charlie—"

"I don't want to hear it." I turned back and faced the front of the room.

I tried not to think about what had just happened, but the conversation kept playing in my head. Was Teo out of my league? *Don't,* I told myself. Confidence was everything, and I had more than my fair share of it. I was not about to let J.D. squash it to pieces. But what if Teo felt the same way? *Charlie! Stop. If he does, then he isn't the guy for you.* Yet I was still getting worked up. Over *J.D.*?! Who cared what *he* thought? *Teo* was clearly into me. *Teo* thought I was attractive. *Teo* was going out of his way to impress me.

"Charlie." J.D. had moved to the seat behind me.

"What?" I snapped.

"You took that totally the wrong way. I wasn't talking about appearances. You're one of the best-looking girls in school."

I turned around and raised an eyebrow at him. Now he was laying it on way too thick.

"Seriously. That's not what I was saying. At all."

Maybe I had jumped to conclusions, but for some unknown reason, it bothered me that J.D. thought that about me.

"Then what are you trying to say?"

"Well, first to clarify. You really are pretty. You are also really stubborn, orderly, rules oriented, and—"

"Great apology you have going on here, J.D."

He laughed. "I'm just saying that yes, both you and Teo are very smart and successful and *attractive* . . ." I rolled my eyes at him. "But you're also really different. It's just, he has a lot going on, he likes to have fun, and he might tend to focus more on himself."

"So you're saying he's self-absorbed." J.D. might not have been able to be blunt, but I had no problem doing it.

"He's my cousin, so I'm not going to put it that way, but . . ."

"Well, then he and I should be a perfect match, huh? Didn't you say I was all about myself?"

"I was just giving you a hard time. It's kind of fun pushing your buttons."

"Yeah, tons of fun." At least he'd found something he excelled at. "But you don't have to worry. I can handle myself." I put my hands around the box Teo gave me. "Besides, a selfish guy does not go out and find kitten marshmallows for someone else."

"Okay." He held up his hands in defeat. "You're right. I was just trying to help."

He looked upset, and I realized I had to let him off the hook. My reaction had been way overboard. He had just gotten to me. "I know, thank you. And you are helping me, and you can't stop. I have no idea what else to get Teo."

"I'll come up with something," he said as he moved back to his own seat.

"Perfect," I said, because Teo and I were on a roll, and there was no way I was letting it slow down.

If anything, it was time to up my game. And I was going to start right after class.

Twenty-One

"Teo," I called out as soon as I spotted him.

He walked over and leaned against the wall with one knee bent. He seriously looked like he could be in an ad for jeans or cologne. "Hey," he said.

Confidence, I reminded myself. *Nerves of steel.* I just needed to pretend I was in a flirting competition, because if there was one thing about me, I did not play to lose. I could do this. "Guess what my Secret Santa brought me?" I said.

"Hmm," he said. "Do I get a clue?"

"It's just the *cutest* gift in the whole world," I answered and opened the box. "I think my Secret Santa has pretty amazing taste."

"That he does."

Okay, he wanted to be cocky. Bring it on. Two could play

that game. "Well, he does have someone pretty stupendous to shop for."

"True," he said, and I'm pretty sure my whole face lit up. He looked like he was about to say something else, but then his focus shifted to something behind me. I turned. It wasn't a something. It was a some*one*.

J.D.

Teo pointed to my present. "Did you see this?" Teo asked J.D. as he exited the classroom. "Santa is totally nailing it."

"Well, that is his job," J.D. said.

"Which he is excelling at," I said, trying to redirect the conversation back to me. I held the box out to Teo. "Want one?"

He picked one out and bit into it, and I never really thought of eating as sexy, but watching Teo, I was beginning to change my mind. He had the nicest lips I'd ever seen. I wanted to reach out and touch them. I wondered what they would be like to kiss.

"So," Teo said, which reminded me to look at his eyes, not his mouth, "getting a gift like this—does it mean you've been naughty or nice?"

"It's marshmallows, not coal," J.D. answered for me, despite my glare in his direction, "so I'd say nice."

"Well, it's always the nice ones you have to watch out for, don't you?" Teo said, while J.D. groaned.

Teo was trying to get a reaction out of me. Well, it was my turn to get one out of him. I was serious about playing to win. "I guess you'll just have to wait and see," I said. Then I gave Teo a wink and turned and walked away.

Did I really just say that? Did I really just do that? Oh my God. I did. Okay, just roll with it. *Play it cool. Do not turn back around. Stand straight. Head high. Make him watch you walk away.* After I made it to the end of the hall and turned into the next corridor, I paused to catch my breath. Seconds later, a hand touched my shoulder.

No way! Teo had come after me. Yes!

"Following me?" I said, making my voice as sultry as possible.

"Actually . . ."

I turned around. "Oh." I dropped the fake voice. "It's you." It wasn't Teo. It was J.D.

"Well, hello to you, too," he said, and adjusted his bag on his arm.

"I'm sorry, I didn't mean it like that. I just thought it was . . . It doesn't matter."

"I just want to make sure you had all the details for tonight," J.D. said.

"Meet at Teo's at seven. That's what you said earlier, right?"

"Yeah," he said, and started walking down the hall. "And Teo told you about the dressing up?"

"The *what?*" I ran to catch him.

"The dressing up. You know, like Santa, a snowman, reindeer, elves, that kind of thing."

"No, no, no," I said, matching his pace. "You have to be kidding." I was not a dress-up type of person. Halloween was one of my least favorite holidays. I only dressed up as a kid because I knew it was the way to get candy, but even then I hated it and went as something real like a doctor or a lab tech or Albert Einstein.

"Nope, every year. Teo loves this kind of thing. He gets super into it."

"Seriously? Why?"

"Why does he do anything? You're asking this about a guy who loves the eighties? I can't figure him out, either. I just know if you want to impress him, you should dress up."

This was horrible. I wanted to wear something cute and flirty, not something reminiscent of Frosty the Snowman. "I don't have a costume."

He stopped in front of his classroom. "I'll tell you what, come by my place beforehand. I'll help you, and I'll show you what I have in mind for your next Teo gift."

"I don't know."

"Do you want to impress Teo or not?" he asked.

I did, and I guess it didn't matter what I wore if it brought me closer to him. "Fine, I'll be there at six."

I just hoped this wasn't a huge mistake.

Twenty-Two

"Ho! Ho! Ho!" J.D. said while holding his stomach when I showed up at his house. He was wearing a Santa suit. "Ready to get decked out?" he asked.

No, no I was not. He looked ridiculous, and pretty soon so would I. I shook my head at him. "You look . . ."

"Dashingly handsome?"

"Not the words I was going for."

"Festive?" he tried.

"More like goofy."

He put his hands on his hips and feigned indignation in what had to be the worst Santa voice I'd ever heard. "Where's your Christmas spirit?" he asked. "Ho! Ho! Ho!"

I held back a laugh. If I didn't, I'd be hearing that horrible impression all night long. "Over at Teo's," I said, reminding him and myself why I was doing this. "Where are your parents?"

"They left for Boston this afternoon to go pick up my sister. They decided to make a whole long weekend out of it. Won't be back till Sunday."

"They trusted you with the house to yourself?"

"Why wouldn't they?" he asked.

I raised an eyebrow. I wasn't about to give him another one of my lists, this one detailing how he did not seem like the responsible type, not when he was helping me, but he knew what I was thinking.

"You really think highly of me, don't you?" he asked, bringing over a large bag.

"I think you're fine." Not that I'd admit it to him, but the truth was, J.D. was growing on me.

"Well, isn't that glowing praise," he said. "Especially when I have this for you." He took a piece of paper out of his big old Santa pocket. "It's just a mock-up, but I can make up a real one if you like it."

I took the paper. It was a baseball card, only Teo was the player featured on it.

"It's a picture from last season. I figured he'd like seeing himself as one of the pros."

"J.D., this is a really great idea, thank you."

He shrugged. "I'll print it out on card stock, make it more like the real thing."

"You really are like Santa." I studied the card. "Teo is going to love this. Should I make this the grand finale present?"

"Nah, I have something better in mind for that."

"What?" I asked.

"Santa can't give away his secrets," he said in his horrible Santa voice again, and then he took his hands and shook his belly.

"Please," I said, half laughing, half cringing, "do yourself—and me—a favor and never do that voice again."

"What voice? This is how I speak."

This was going to be a long, long night. "Okay, *Santa*, just tell me, when do I get to find out Teo's final gift?"

"Next Wednesday after the *Sentinel* meeting—"

"There is no *Sentinel* meeting since the paper is coming out that Friday and we're having the party. *Which*, FYI, you would have known if you had shown up on time yesterday."

"This is how you talk to Santa?" he said in mock disgust as he rummaged through the mystery bag he had in front of him. "At this rate, you, not to mention poor Teo, may wind up with a sack of coal."

"You're right, you're right," I conceded. "I'm sorry. What were you saying?"

"That Wednesday after school, you and I are going to go on a little adventure."

"I don't do adventures. I hate them."

"You'll like this one," he assured me. "It's to get Teo's final gift." He was back to his normal voice. "And trust me, he will go nuts over it."

"Can you at least give me an idea where we're going? I like to plan."

"You?" he asked. "I wouldn't have known. All I'll say is just be prepared for a long night."

Great, a long night going on some unknown adventure to places unknown. This had better be the best gift in the history of gifts, because getting it sounded like a Christmas nightmare.

"It'll be fun, I promise."

He had come through for me so far. "Okay, I will trust you. Don't make me regret it."

"Yes, ma'am," he said and saluted.

I shook my head at him again and then glanced at the time. "We need to hurry up, I don't want to be late for Teo's."

"We're fine."

Maybe I trusted him with picking out presents, but definitely not with time. Fine to J.D. meant showing up whenever it suited him. Fine to me was punctuality.

"So what do you want to be?" he asked, still fishing through the bag.

"What? I have no idea. It doesn't make a difference."

"Mrs. Claus then?" he said, pulling out a little bonnet.

Maybe it made a little bit of a difference. "I don't think so." J.D. was not the cousin I wanted to look like I was paired up with. "What's Teo going as?"

"Ralphie from *A Christmas Story*. Complete with pink one-piece bunny pajamas."

"Stop, he is not."

J.D. sat down on the couch. "No, he is. It was a dare, and he said if anyone could pull the costume off it was him." That did seem like something Teo would say. I could almost picture the little glint in his eye as he accepted the challenge. But it still seemed out there.

"He's really going as Ralphie?"

"He really is, and that's why I think you need to step up your game. Forget Mrs. Claus. Forget Rudolph. Forget the tradition. I think you need to go all in, show that Christmas spirit, *be* that Christmas spirit."

"What does that even mean?"

He pulled out an artificial wreath, with a ribbon tied around it. "It means this."

I shot him a look. "And what am I supposed to do with that?"

"You wear it," he said placing it on top of my head, making sure the bow that was attached to it was right in front.

"Okay, you know how I said you looked goofy, I look ludicrous."

"That's the whole point. The more you're into it, the more Teo is going to be into *you*."

Then he pulled out a hideous bright-red vest that was not meant for a redhead, and put it on me. "It will fit over your coat," he said.

"Perfect," I said, making sure he didn't miss the sarcasm dripping from my tongue. "You sure costume design isn't in your future?"

He pointed to the bag. "Think you can do better?" Then he broke into a huge grin. "That was a dumb question. Of course you do. You're *Charlie Donovan*."

"Don't you forget it," I told him. Only this time, instead of our normal bickering, this felt different. Like when you joked around with, dare I say, a friend. Wait. Was that possible? The costume was probably just rubbing off on me. "If you're picking my costume," I said, "I think it's only fair that I get to pick yours."

"Deal," he said. "But for the record, we are not even close to done with yours."

"In that case," I said, "I'd better load you up with as much of this stuff as I can." I dug through the bag, and I struck gold. "This. This is the one. You have to put it on." It was a giant felt candy cane costume, with a little round opening at the top for your face and slits for your arms.

He grimaced. "Of course you'd find that one."

"Why do you have this incredibly amazing stuff?"

"My sister used to do holiday plays. This one"—he pointed to the costume—"was one she wrote herself about the adventures of the Sugar Plum Fairy and her best friend, Candy Cane."

"Oh please tell me you played the Sugar Plum Fairy."

"Alas," he said as he hung his head, "I didn't. But . . ." He paused for dramatic effect. "I was their archnemesis, the Tooth Fairy!"

"You were not! Okay, that might be even better. Where's that costume?" I asked.

"You're out of luck. I was eight when I wore it, and I only did the show because my sister and her friend bribed me with as much chocolate as I could eat. I may have wiped my hands on the costume."

"Too bad."

"My mom thought so. She is a saver. She doesn't throw anything out. 'You never know when the perfect occasion will arise to use it again,'" he said, doing another really bad impression.

"You mean like right now!" I handed him the felt suit.

152

He took off his Santa jacket and the pillow he had belted around his waist, which revealed a tight white T-shirt that outlined the muscles on his chest. I realized I was staring and quickly turned away.

"Uh, I might need some help," he said. I looked back to see a felt tube covering his head and the top of his shoulders, with the rest of the costume flapping over to the side.

"You might," I said, not bothering to hide my laughter. I tried pulling the costume down, but I could only get it another few inches. "This is not budging."

He shimmied to try to remove the costume, and he looked like one of those air dancers—the inflatable plastic tube men you see in front of car dealerships.

"Let me get it," I said, and helped free him. His T-shirt lifted slightly. *Seriously, Charlie. Stop looking at J.D.* I made sure to make eye contact. Or I tried to anyway, only this time I got sidetracked by something else. "Your hair." The costume caused some static electricity, and it was sticking out everywhere. I reached out to smooth it down and felt a jolt.

I jumped back slightly, and J.D. smiled. "Does this mean I'm back to Santa?"

"Yes," I said, and handed him his pillow and jacket before I found myself accidentally staring at him again.

"But we still haven't finished you," he said.

"Please don't make me the candy cane."

"Don't worry, you're still Christmas spirit." He looked me over, and I don't know why, but I found myself adjusting my wreath. "I know what's missing," he said. Seconds later, he was attaching a giant blinking Christmas tree pin to my vest. "We're getting there," he said. "Just a few more touches. I know exactly the thing." Then he went back into the bag. He pulled out reindeer ears. "No." He pushed aside a Rudolph nose. "Not right, either." His eyes got wide. "Now these were what I was looking for."

I couldn't see what he had found, but my guess was that I was not going to like it.

Was I ever right.

Twenty-Three

I am taking these things off," I said after I parked in front of Teo's. I glanced in my rearview mirror. J.D. had found elf ears—and not little elf ears, ginormous ones. It was definitely not the look I was going for. "I look like that *Star Trek* guy."

"Spock."

"Yes, how is he supposed to be Christmasy?" I went to take them off.

"Leave them," J.D. said. "They complete the look. Besides, who doesn't love a Christmas elf? And this is nothing compared to bunny pajamas."

He might have been right, but I didn't care. I pulled them off, my hands jingling as I lowered my arm. J.D. had also given me little bell bracelets to wear.

I wanted to look Christmasy cute, not like I belonged on a sci-fi show. The vest and pin over my jacket, the wreath on my head, and the jingle bells were a little over the top. I looked like a Christmas tag sale had exploded all over me, but Teo would hopefully appreciate the effort.

"Say cheese," J.D. said, following me out of the car.

"Put that camera away," I warned him.

"Don't you want a picture with your new boyfriend?"

"I hate having my photo taken, and he's not my . . ."

He snapped the picture before I finished.

We walked up to Teo's. *Remember to smile,* I told myself as I rang the doorbell. *Teo loves this whole costume thing. Show him that you truly are Christmas spirit.*

"Merry Christmas," I said when he opened the door.

Teo just stared at me, his mouth agape. "What the . . . why are . . . ?"

He was wearing perfectly normal, everyday clothes. "You're dressing up, right?" I asked, even though I had a pretty good idea I knew the answer.

"Are you kidding?" Then he started to laugh. Seriously laugh. "Guys, you have got to see this," he called to the people in the house.

For someone who always thought she was so smart, I was incredibly dumb.

I turned to J.D. "You are such a jerk."

Only he was laughing, too. His fake Santa belly was shaking at my expense.

I took off the pin and threw it at him. "I hate you so much."

"You told her to do this?" Teo asked.

Then he high-fived his cousin. I was going to have to seriously reconsider my crush.

"You are both horrible people," I said and started to take the wreath off.

"No, don't take it off, it's cute," Teo said. "Sorry, I shouldn't laugh." But he didn't even try to hide the huge grin on his face. Then three other people—two girls and guy—surrounded him at the door.

"Whoa," one of the girls said, peeking around Teo's left side. She looked familiar. I'd seen her around the halls at school. "Interesting outfit choice."

Then the laughter picked up again.

J.D. was so dead.

"All right, lay off, Heather," he told her and the others after noticing the death rays shooting from my eyes straight at him.

Heather. She was what I wanted to look like today. Cute, with a formfitting dress, and her hair done up to perfection in some sort of elaborate twist. Instead, I looked like a decked-out Pillsbury Doughboy, and *my* hair?! If I took off the wreath, I'd have a rat's nest, and if I left it on, I basically had an actual nest on my head.

How could I have thought Teo was actually going to be dressed as Ralphie?

"Everyone ready?" Teo asked the group in the house. The others went and grabbed their coats.

"So, you finally got someone to dress up with you, huh?" Teo asked J.D. as he stepped outside.

"Excuse me?" I asked.

157

"Every year, he tries to convince us to have some sort of theme," Teo explained.

"And every year, we tell him no way," Heather said, joining us. "Guess you must really like him or something."

"Or something." I wasn't about to explain that I did this in a very misguided attempt to impress Teo.

"All right, guys, and Santa, and . . . what are you?" Teo asked me.

"Christmas spirit," I said flatly.

"Okay." He laughed again. "Christmas spirit, let's go." He put his arm around me. "We're meeting the rest of the group down the street at Polly's. We do the caroling there. They have a whole neighborhood event. You'll love it, Christmas spirit."

Maybe every cloud did have a silver lining. Teo Ortiz had his arm around me! And I more than needed the extra TLC after this humiliation. "What about your parents and Dylan?" I asked. "Aren't they coming?"

"They went with an earlier group that had younger kids. We're the 'teen' group," he said, making quotes with his free hand.

"We're also the pro group," Heather said, sidling up to Teo's other side. "We're in the Aca-mazings—or at least most of us are." The Aca-mazings was the school's a cappella group. No wonder she looked familiar. I had seen her and the rest of her ensemble perform at assemblies a few times. They were really talented.

"I've never seen you sing with them," I told Teo.

"I did it my freshman year."

"He's really amazing. I was so upset when he quit." Heather gave him a little pout, and much to my displeasure, Teo put his other arm around her. She instantly brightened up. "The whole group doesn't come out caroling, so we need some fill-ins. Especially guys. So Teo has been helping us out over the years, and he pulled in J.D."

"Nice," I said, although I was beginning to get uncomfortable. Not just because of the way Heather was looking up at Teo like a lovesick puppy, but because a realization hit. These people could *really* sing. *All of them.* All of them but *me.*

I turned to J.D., my one last hope. "Do you have a good voice, too?"

"It's okay."

"He's being modest," Heather answered. "He'd totally make the group if he tried out."

Perfect. Just what my night needed.

All I wanted to do was impress Teo, but I was just going from one embarrassment to another. I thought this was going to be a fun, friendly caroling night where no one would notice or care about my off-key singing. I didn't expect everyone to be terrific vocalists. I mean, seriously, what were the odds that Teo was going to be exceptional at absolutely everything he tried? So, basically, they were all going to sound like angels, while I sounded like a cat in heat. Worse, I'd probably make the cat seem like it had an ounce of talent.

But I momentarily forgot all of that when we arrived at Polly's. "Wow," I gasped.

"Pretty amazing, huh?" Teo said.

That was an understatement. It was an actual winter wonderland. I didn't know neighborhoods like this even existed. It was a cul-de-sac that had been transformed into a little Christmas village. First there were the decorations—lights circled just about every tree, telephone pole, and mailbox, fake icicles hung from houses, candles were on windowsills, and there were holiday displays on several lawns—everything from a Nativity scene to Santa and his reindeer. Then there were the sounds. Sure, there was Christmas music playing, but what really caught me was the buzz of the street. I had never seen so many neighbors outside at once. Everyone was talking to one another, laughing, sharing food. There was a line of tables that had Christmas cookies and other treats on it, an actual food truck where someone was handing out hot chocolate, and one person even had a barbecue set up. The smell wafting from it was delicious. "What is that?" I asked.

"Chestnuts," Teo said.

No way. This place actually had chestnuts roasting on an open fire. I was wrong; this place wasn't just a Christmas village, it was Christmas heaven.

"Ever had them?" he asked.

I shook my head.

"Well, I think it's one of those things Christmas spirit should experience," he said. Then he took my hand and led me to the barbecue.

He was holding my hand! Was there a place even better than heaven? Because that's where I was right now.

He dropped my hand to give me a chestnut, but I could still feel the warmth from where he touched me.

"Well," he asked after I bit into one. "What do you think?"

"It's perfect." And I wasn't just talking about the chestnut, which had a smoky taste mixed with a twinge of sweetness.

"I'm glad you like it," he said. "I—"

"Teo," a girl called out and then ran over and gave him a big hug, interrupting us. Heather, J.D., the rest of the group from Teo's, and several others were right behind her.

"Hey, Polly," Teo said, hugging her back.

Their embrace went on way too long. I wasn't the only one who noticed. Heather shot her a nasty look. Clearly, I wasn't the only one vying for Teo's attention. But I was the one whose hand he had held only minutes ago!

"We want to get started," she said.

And then I remembered I was also the only one who was going to look like a fool in mere moments. I couldn't sing with these people. What was I going to do?

Lip-sync. It was my only choice.

Heather passed around a song order list, and we headed to the center of the cul-de-sac. "We don't actually have the sheet music. We've been doing this so long, we kinda have everything down."

"That's okay," I said. I actually knew the words to most Christmas songs. My problem wasn't the lyrics, it was keeping a tune.

As the crowd saw us getting ready, they turned off the music and hushed one another. A bunch of kids sat on the curb, their parents on folding chairs behind them.

When Heather introduced the group, there was thunderous applause. This was a huge deal to these people. I was so out of my league.

Yet somehow I wound up in the front row next to Teo. "Just jump in wherever you see fit," he whispered to me.

The only place I fit was back in my bed under my covers.

The first song was "Do You Hear What I Hear?" and when Heather said they had it down, she was not kidding.

First J.D. and one of the other guys started spitting out beats, then the others started singing. Some had the main verse, some echoed after them, but they all harmonized and sounded like they should be doing this for a living. They even had movements down. I did my own choreography. I shuffled away from Teo and to the back of the group. There was no way I was going to jump into that. It would have been like a third grader who just started flute lessons jumping into a performance at Carnegie Hall. It just didn't happen, not unless you wanted to get ridiculed off the stage.

The song lasted about five minutes, and by the end, any neighbor who hadn't come by for the performance before certainly was coming over now. Not that I blamed them. It was a killer show. I'd have come and watched it, too. In fact, at that very moment, I wished I *was* with the spectators instead of the singers.

There was another wave of applause, and J.D. moved closer to me. "Why aren't you singing?"

"I am."

"*Charlie.*"

How could he tell? "Fine, because you didn't tell me this was the Christmas caroler all-star team," I hissed.

"No one cares if you can sing; that's not what this is about," he said.

"Right, just like no one cares if they win the championship football game, or science fair, or place first in their class."

"It's not the same thing," he said, but it was hard to take him seriously in that Santa getup. Not that I was one to talk.

Before I could prove to him I was right, the group started up again with "The Twelve Days of Christmas." I had always loved that song, only now I just wished it would hurry up and end.

I dutifully mouthed along all the words, but then my cover was blown. When we got to the third day of Christmas, Teo started pointing at people in the group for each gift, and they each sang that line by themselves, while everyone else harmonized and did their beat thing in the background. *Please don't point to me, please don't point to me.* Normally, I liked to be called on, but that was in school, where I had the answers. Here it felt like I was being sent to walk the plank.

I made it through the first three days of Christmas.

Then it was the fourth day. I mouthed along to *On the fourth day of Christmas my true love sent to me* then braced myself as Teo made his choice. I was safe; he picked J.D. for *four calling birds.*

But I really panicked when the next verse started. I'd be able to talk-sing through *seven swans a-swimming* and *six geese a-laying*—but five, five was *five golden rings.* And you had to be able to carry a tune for that. It was high and drawn out. *Do not pick me, do not pick me, do not pick me.*

Apparently Teo and I needed to work on subliminal messages, because he seemed to mistake my panic-stricken look for one of budding showmanship—and pointed at me for number five. "Five golden rings," I whispered.

Teo wrinkled his forehead but just kept going. I had to do that *seven* more times?! I looked around. There had to be a way to escape.

"Own it," J.D. said. "Let people hear you."

"Easy for you to say. You can sing."

"You want Teo? He doesn't want scared and meek. And last time I checked, that wasn't you. Besides, the night is going to be a lot more fun if you actually take part."

I didn't have much time to make up my mind because the sixth verse had started, and seconds later it was back to me. *Just do it,* I commanded myself. "Five golden rings," I sang way too loudly, my voice cracking in the middle of *golden.* I could hear people laughing, both the group I was with and the people watching.

J.D. was smiling while he did his line. "See," he said afterward, "isn't that better?"

Sometimes I seriously wondered if he was from another planet. "No, that was not better. Didn't you hear everyone's reaction?"

"Because you went all in. They weren't laughing at you, they were laughing *with* you. You have fun, they'll have fun. Trust me."

I wasn't so sure. But it wasn't like I had time to weigh the pros and cons. It was my turn again. "Five golden rings," I sang out, attempting to take J.D's advice. I wanted to seem like I was proud of my off-key voice, but it was hard. I felt so self-conscious. But what if J.D. was right? Maybe this was like one of those sketch comedy shows where the actors break character and start laughing, and everyone laughs with them.

"That's better," J.D. said. "But really go for it next time. Don't you see? You're giving people the ability to just enjoy themselves. Not everyone in this audience can sing. They're like you."

"Thanks," I said.

"What I mean is, they love carols and they love singing, and they want to see someone up here doing that, too. Not everything has to be by-the-letter perfect. Seriously, just let yourself have fun with it."

Well, it was either that or suffer. So fun it was. When it came around to my turn again, not only did I sing my line loudly, horribly, and off-key, but I threw in hand gestures. I raised my hands in the air and shook them with each word.

This time I got more laughs. Even Teo was smiling.

"See, was that so bad?" J.D. asked.

I waved my hand in a so-so motion.

When my turn came around again, J.D. joined me in the hand motions, and the next time, Teo did, too. By the time we reached the last verse—the twelfth day of Christmas—not only were all of the carolers doing it, but so was the audience, who also joined me in belting out my thoroughly off-key line.

It really did feel like they had my back. And when the applause came, I felt like some of it was meant for me, too.

J.D. caught me smiling. "I told you it was about more than having a good voice," he said. "See, you really are bringing out the Christmas spirit after all. I picked the right costume for you."

"Don't even start with that," I said.

"Sorry, I thought dressing up would be funny, and," he said, patting his Santa belly, "it wasn't like I made you do it alone."

"You should have told me we'd be the only ones."

"Then you never would have done it."

"No kidding," I said.

"Admit it, you are having fun, costume and all," he said. When I didn't answer, he said, "Okay, well then this is for you. I'll be right back, and you'd better sing this time."

He went up to the front of the group before they could start their next song.

Oh no. What was he doing? If he was asking them to give me a solo, I didn't care if he was dressed as Santa, Mrs. Claus was going to have to start shopping for a new husband.

"Go with me," he told them and then turned to the crowd. "We're going to go a little off schedule right now, because we want all of you to get involved. So get your voices ready, we need you to join in. We're going to do 'Here Comes Santa Claus,' and I want to hear all of you!" With that, he gestured for all of us carolers to mingle with the crowd, and then he started singing. Pretty soon everyone was. I had never seen anything like it. Household after household coming together, having fun, laughing, smiling, caroling.

J.D. was back by my side. He picked up my arm and shook it so the bells would ring. "I don't hear you," he whispered.

I figured maybe just this once he was right. Maybe scrapping the plan was the way to go. So I projected my voice and let it join the others. I even let Santa guide me around to all the little kids outside, with him shaking his belly and me letting my jingle bells chime. I might not have had the best voice, but I did have the Christmas spirit after all.

Twenty-Four

"All right, all right, all right, I admit it, it was fun. There, are you happy?" I asked.

The whole walk back to Teo's, J.D. had been gloating about how, despite my utter humiliation, he turned it into a great evening.

"That doesn't mean you are off the hook," I warned him. "But I did manage to have a couple of moments with Teo even in this getup . . . so I don't entirely hate you anymore."

"Good to know," he said.

"Seriously, though." I nudged him lightly with my elbow. "Thank you. This was a fun night." It really was. I hadn't been feeling especially Christmasy this year, and this gave me the boost I needed.

"Well, you know," he said, "I hear the Aca-mazings need a new member. Should I tell them you're in?"

"Only if they want to lose every competition."

"They may be able to deal with that—but you?" He shook his head at me. "Don't think so."

That was more than a little true. "Okay, but it's not my fault. I was born this way."

"What way?"

"Liking to win. You know, I was even Baby New Year. Coming in first from day one." I was delivered right at the stroke of midnight.

"This explains a lot," he said, laughing. "January first, huh?"

"Yep, right when everyone is tired out from partying the night before, not to mention Christmas."

"That kind of sucks."

I shrugged. "It kind of does. It's like I don't have a day of my own. The second or the third would have been preferable, but there's not much I can do about it now."

"Wait, something you can't control?" He put on an expression of mock horror. "How do you handle it?"

"Well," I said, feigning complete seriousness. "By taking it out on the school paper's photo editor, of course."

"Now that I believe."

Just then a few flakes hit my arms. "Oh. My. God! J.D.," I practically shrieked. "It's snowing!"

He put out his arms. "You're right."

It was only a few flakes at first, but then it picked up. The first snow of the season. "I love this," I said and started spinning as J.D. stuck out his tongue trying to catch some snowflakes.

The two of us had to have made the most absurd sight.

Santa and Christmas spirit getting excited by the snow, but the thought just made me smile. It felt right. I couldn't picture it any other way.

This capped the night perfectly. It was making me visibly giddy. I was spinning so fast, I knocked into J.D. We both started laughing. Then he took my hands and started twirling with me. If one of us had let go, we would have wound up flying into the hedges. I let out a squeal as we spun at warp speed.

Teo turned around. "What is going on back there?" he asked.

J.D. and I stopped circling as Teo looked from his cousin to me.

"Just taking in the snow," I said. The way he was staring at us . . . NO! Did he think I liked his *cousin*? I was so stupid. I should have been paying attention to Teo. I moved to his side. "It's so beautiful, right?"

"It is." Heather butted in from Teo's other side. Then she wiped some snow out of his hair, and the lightheartedness I felt just seconds earlier floated away.

When we got to his house, we all kind of stood there. I was waiting for Heather to leave before I budged, but she didn't seem to be going anywhere.

It was getting awkward, and I didn't want to look like I was a hanger-on-er. That did not bode well for my mission to get Teo to take me to Noelle's party, so I said my good-byes. Operation Secret Santa would have to pick up another day. "Do you guys need a ride?" I asked J.D. and Heather.

Unfortunately, only J.D. took me up on it. Heather was hanging back.

"Hey," Teo called out to his cousin as we headed to the car. "My mom wants me to ask you if I should bring anything tomorrow."

"What's tomorrow?" Heather asked.

"My parents are gone for the weekend, and Teo and I are going to hang out," J.D. told her.

Her mouth opened. "You're having a party and didn't invite me?"

"It's not a party," he said.

"It could be," Teo volunteered. "Your parents aren't home."

Heather clapped her hands and jumped up and down. "Party at J.D.'s house, party at J.D.'s house!"

"Shh," he warned her. "There is no party. My mom will kill me."

"Not if she doesn't find out," Teo said.

"Can we all keep our voices down, please? Come on, Teo," J.D. warned him. "I do not need your parents hearing this. And you know my mom finds out everything."

"What if we kept it small?" Teo pressed. "What do you think, Charlie? Aren't you up for a party?"

I saw the panic in J.D.'s eyes. I knew he really didn't want anything at his house, but I also saw the pleading look in Teo's. He wanted me to help convince his cousin.

I knew the right thing was to defend J.D., but I really wanted another night where I could hang out with Teo. One where we could actually talk. "Something small could be nice."

"Charlie!" J.D. bemoaned.

"Sorry," I mouthed to him so Teo couldn't see. But he knew I was striving for more Teo time, and this was the opportunity I needed. "We can all bring stuff," I said, trying to ease some of his fears. "You won't have to do *anything*."

"I've got just the thing," Teo said, his smile widening.

Meantime, J.D. looked tense. "*If* we do this, it's just going to be us and a few others, so don't invite anyone, Teo."

"Just a couple," he said. "Maybe a few people from the team. Plus, Cecilia, Polly—"

"No," J.D. said. "No one. Seriously. This will be the four of us." He looked at me and sighed. "And my neighbor and her boyfriend. That's it. Okay?"

"Okay, okay," Teo said.

"And just so you all know, this will be the lamest party ever," J.D. warned us.

He *really* didn't want this, but he had caved. And it was just six people. It wasn't even truly a party; it was more like a tiny gathering.

"I think something low-key sounds good," I said.

"And," J.D. said, finally starting to smile. "Since it's *my* party, I say we all dress up. Ugly. Holiday. Sweaters. If you're not wearing one, you don't get to come in."

This was his revenge on me for siding with his cousin. He knew I'd want to wear something cute. Whatever, I could make it work.

"I have the perfect thing," Heather said. Of course she did.

When we finally got in the car, I turned to J.D. "Ugly Christmas sweaters? Really?"

"If I'm stuck doing this, my rules." His dimple was on full display.

"Your rules. Then can we uninvite Heather?" I didn't want to compete for Teo's attention.

"I want to uninvite everyone. My parents will freak out if they know I'm having people over while they're gone."

"I'm sorry." I felt guilty. "But it's just six of us—including you. And I'm going to help you with everything. Food, supplies, on me. I'll even get there early to set up. Whatever you want. Your parents won't even know I was there."

"It's not you I'm worried about. When Teo is in a group, he likes to make things interesting."

"Interesting isn't bad. And he was fine tonight."

"Yeah," he said, "you're right. It's probably nothing."

"Thank you so much for doing this."

"We are even now," he said, tapping my wreath. "You can't hold this against me."

"Absolutely," I assured him. If dressing up like the Ghost of Embarrassing Christmases Past ensured me a night with Teo, then it was all worth it.

Twenty-Five

After school, Morgan and I stopped by the Super Shop Now. It was one of those giant stores that had everything from food and everyday household items to books, electronics, toys, and clothes. As I picked up supplies for the party, Morgan checked out the sweaters.

We met at the checkout line. "Got it," she said, holding up a giant blue sweater.

"That is way too big for you."

"That's the point," she said. "Ira and I are going to wear it together. If I rip the collar open, both of our heads will fit."

"You will be attached to him all night," I reminded her.

"I don't mind."

"Remember that when you have to go to the bathroom," I warned her.

"It's a sweater," she said. "We'll have shirts on underneath.

We don't have to wear it the entire evening. J.D. is not going to kick us out if we take it off."

"Maybe not you." I wasn't so sure that was the case for me. I took the sweater from her and put it in the cart. "A two-person sweater is odd, for sure, but I don't know if it classifies as ugly."

"And that's why I was up late last night making felt cutouts of a menorah, dreidel, and the Star of David." They were all symbols of Hanukkah.

"You're going to sew them on?" I asked.

"As soon as I get home," she said.

"Maybe I should have asked you to make me one, too. You remember what my ugly Christmas sweater looks like?"

I grimaced, and Morgan laughed. "It's funny," she said as we moved up in line.

"Well, it's not like J.D. gave me much time to find anything better. I looked at the ones here, but they're not ugly enough, so I don't have any other options. So much for being sexy."

"Hey, the Christmas spirit costume ended up winning over Teo, so this will, too." She started laughing. "That still cracks me up every time I think of it. When you texted me you needed to dress up for the caroling, I thought you meant a nice skirt or a dress. I can't believe you actually got in a costume. I can't even get you to try on anything on Halloween."

"Tell me about it, and now I'm basically doing it twice in one week."

"But for a good reason," she said.

"Yes," I agreed, "and don't forget your job tonight."

"I know, I know, Ira and I have to make sure you get plenty

of alone time with Teo and we have to distract Heather if she tries to—" She stopped talking and her posture went rigid. "Do not look to your right," she whispered.

I know she warned me not to, but I looked anyway and wound up making direct eye contact with, of all people, Zakiyah. Why hadn't I listened to Morgan?

"Trolling the store to find someone to pretend to be your date for Noelle's party?" Zakiyah called out to me. The two girls with her laughed.

"I have a date."

"Right, the most 'perfect' date," she said, making air quotes. "Maybe you can try and create one for your next science project, because that's the only way you'll land that kind of guy."

Morgan sneered at Zakiyah and then ushered me to the cashier. "Ignore her," she said. "Let's just pay and get out of here."

I nodded. Morgan was right; I was not going to let Zakiyah goad me. I was going to use it as extra motivation. Pretty soon Teo would be mine, and I'd be the one laughing.

I opened the car trunk so we could put the party stuff in.

"What's this?" Morgan asked, pulling out a small wrapped package.

"The Donkey Kong key chain for Teo." I threw it in there so I wouldn't forget it next week.

"You didn't give that to him today?"

"Nope, I have that scheduled for Monday," I told her.

"Oh." She ever so slightly scrunched her eyebrows, but I caught it.

"What? What's wrong?" I specifically chose Monday so he'd

get a gift then, one on Wednesday, and then the big reveal gift on Friday. It was spaced perfectly.

"There's nothing wrong, but it would give him something to think about over the weekend," she said, placing the final bag in the trunk. "Plus, you're seeing him tonight, so you could have dropped more hints about how someone who got him such personal gifts must really be incredible."

I hadn't considered that. The more Teo's Secret Santa was on his mind, the better.

The whole ride back to Morgan's, I couldn't drop the thought. I should have given him the present today. Then when he saw me at the party, it would be another thing to talk about. I kicked myself for not thinking of it sooner.

It wasn't like the day was exactly over, I still had plenty of time. I could drop it off at his house on my way back home. It would only take a few minutes, and I still had three hours until I needed to be at J.D.'s—and that was with me arriving super early to set up. It was a no-brainer.

I was going to do it! Zakiyah was going to be eating her words soon.

I dropped Morgan off and then headed for Teo's. I was all set, but as I got closer to his house, I began second-guessing my decision to go at all. Maybe my original plan had been better. Maybe waiting until Monday at school was the way to go.

I turned onto his street and pulled over at a random house. I couldn't very well park right in front of Teo's house. What if someone was home? I could just picture one of his parents spotting me. *I promise, I'm not a stalker lingering outside your house. Just leaving your son a little present*. Yeah, that didn't seem strange at all.

The more I thought about it, the more ridiculous it seemed. I could wait to give him the present.

No, Charlie. You are already here. You already adjusted your plan once. Just do it.

I took a deep breath and got out of the car. I'd just run. Leave the gift between the screen and main door and go. Easy peasy.

I made sure the coast was clear and bolted for his porch. I was practically out of breath by the time I made it up the three front stairs. I really needed to schedule in some exercise time. Although it was probably more nerves than lack of physical prowess that was causing the breathing issues.

Doubt flooded me. What if no one found the present until tomorrow? That would defeat the whole purpose of making a special trip. Or what if it snowed more and my gift fell, got buried, and was shoveled away, never to be seen again?

Stop, Charlie. Someone will be walking up the porch later. It's not even five. Teo's walkway was shoveled from yesterday's snow, and the forecasters weren't predicting another storm. Do not freak out over nothing.

With that thought, I opened up the screen, placed the present halfway in, and let the door shut back on it. But as it closed, the door let out a loud squeak.

"Mom?" Teo called out.

I froze.

Why was he here? Why couldn't he be volunteering? This was bad. What was I supposed to do? Each second seemed like hours.

I had to make up my mind. Time was ticking. Did I stay there and face him? Or run?

I wasn't ready for this. Impulse kicked in. Fight or flight, and apparently I was all about flight. I took off running.

I heard the door squeak again, and I dived behind a bush.

"Hello?" Teo said.

Crap, crap, crap, crap, crap, crap, crap.

I made a mistake. A big one. Why hadn't I just stayed there? This was definitely among the top three dumb moves of my life. Of course Teo was going to know it was me hiding out as soon as I revealed myself as his Secret Santa next week. I left the Donkey Kong key chain at the door. I could have just stayed there and said I wanted to see if there was anything special he wanted me to pick up for the party. Or confessed that I was the one who pulled his name and that I wanted to surprise him with his next gift. But no, I made the wise choice to crouch behind a bush. This was why I planned things out. *This* was why I didn't make rash decisions. If I had actually spent any real time going over scenarios, I would not have been in this predicament.

"Who's there?" Teo asked, his voice getting closer. Of course it was. The snow on the ground made a trail to my location.

I wasn't sure I believed human spontaneous combustion could actually take place, but if there was a time to prove the theory, it was now.

"I said, who's there?"

I had no choice. I was about to be discovered, so I stood up.

"Charlie?" he asked. He looked totally confused. Not that I

could blame him. It wasn't every day that you found someone from school hiding in your shrubbery.

"Hi." I gave a little wave.

"What are you doing here?"

I really should have waited for Monday to do this.

My mind raced. *Oh, you know, a little light stalking. Checking on your forsythia bush, stupendous job on the hedging. Sleep-walking, don't mind me.* But I went with the truth. "I wanted to drop off your Secret Santa gift."

"You're my Secret Santa?" he asked, rubbing his shoulder. He was clearly, and understandably, trying to make sense of it all.

"Surprise," I said. I felt so self-conscious. I wiped my jacket and jeans with my hands to get rid of the snow, hoping I wasn't an absolute mess.

"Why did you hide?" he asked.

I shrugged. "I didn't want to give away that I was your Secret Santa. You weren't supposed to find out yet." It wasn't a complete lie.

"Right," he said, his voice softer.

I didn't know what else to say, so I just stood there wishing I had one of those Harry Potter invisibility cloaks scientists were working on and braced for the worst.

Only it didn't come.

"So," Teo said, and then broke into one of his award-worthy smiles, "what did you get me?" I instantly felt a hundred percent lighter.

Maybe this wasn't going to be such a bad thing after all. "You'll have to open it." I meant to say it in a flirty voice, but honestly, I was so frazzled I sounded more like Elmo from *Sesame Street*, high-pitched and slightly goofy.

I could tell he was holding back a laugh. "Okay," he said, and looked toward his door. Lying not too far away from it was my present. It must have fallen to the side when he came outside. He walked over, picked it up, and shook it. I followed him to the walkway to get out of the snow, but I made sure to keep a decent amount of distance. I really didn't want him to think I was a stalker.

"Should I guess?" he asked.

"You can try." But I was fairly certain he wouldn't figure it out.

"Okay," he said, and came back down the stairs.

"Is it a gift card?"

I shook my head.

He took a step closer. "Is it chocolate?"

"Strike two."

The next thing I knew Teo was so close there was only an inch of space between us. My equilibrium was going way off kilter, and I had to remind myself to breathe like a normal person.

"Is it maybe . . ." He lifted the present above my head. "Mistletoe?"

It wasn't, but now I kind of wished it was. I shook my head again.

He lowered the gift back down and winked at me. "Too bad."

Wait. Did that mean he wanted to kiss me?!!!

"I guess I'm just going to have to look," he said, but the whole time he never took his eyes off me.

Okay, it was totally freezing outside, but I was burning up, and there was no question as to why.

Oh my God. What if, after he opened the gift, he actually *did* kiss me? Was my breath okay? Were my lips chapped? My lips hadn't touched anyone else's since Ajay. Did I even remember how to do it right?

He ripped off the wrapping paper, and just like that the mood changed from swoonworthy romance to childlike glee, and I was smacked back to reality.

"No way," he said, and tore into the packaging so he could remove the key chain. "I didn't know they made these. They have tiny controls and everything. Charlie, this is awesome." His face lit up. "Thank you."

"You're welcome."

Then the totally unexpected happened.

Teo leaned in and gave me a light kiss on the cheek.

It wasn't exactly the kiss I'd been daydreaming about, but it was a very good start.

I got to feel Teo Ortiz's lips on me, and I definitely wanted it to happen again!

Twenty-Six

"W hy are you floating?" my mother said when I walked in.
"Mom!" I hadn't expected to see her there. I thought
she was working tonight. "You're home."

"I am, and where have you been?" She could sense I was
flying high about something. I knew it was just a peck on the
cheek, but it was sweet and perfect, and I was going to get to see
Teo again tonight.

"Just dropping off a Secret Santa gift." The memory made
me smile even wider. Going out with Teo wasn't just some wish
anymore, it was a distinct possibility.

"Well, I can't wait to hear all about it," she said.

"I thought you were doing a double tonight."

"Someone was able to take the second shift, so I thought I'd
get to spend some time with my daughter."

"That's great!" I told her, but then I realized what that meant.

I'd have to choose between hanging out with my mom and going to the party. I had to admit I was torn. I really wanted to spend time with her. I did. *But* I also really wanted to see Teo. Not to mention, I promised J.D. I'd take care of everything for the party. Since I helped coerce him into throwing it, I kind of owed him. How could I back out of that?

Once again my mom could tell something was up. "Don't worry," she said. "I also need to catch up on my sleep. So how about we hang out, have some dinner, you fill me in on this person who's making you smile—and then you go to that party you told me about the other day, and I will have a date with my bed?"

Okay, my day started out rocky with running into Zakiyah and hiding in a bush, but it turned into the most amazingly amazing one. An unbelievable moment with Teo, a party to look forward to, and getting to spend time with my mom when she didn't seem half asleep? Definitely on the nice list! Mom and I stuffed our faces with boxed macaroni and cheese (one of the dishes both of us could actually cook), talked about my crush (minus me rigging the drawing), how J.D. (the guy I complained about all year) was helping me, her work, and what we hoped Santa would bring us.

The time flew by. I hated how when you wanted to savor moments, they went by at the speed of light and when you wished they'd hurry up, they felt like an eternity.

"Have fun tonight," my mom said. "And don't stay out too late."

"I won't," I promised. I grabbed my sweater and then booked it to J.D.'s.

When I got to his house, I carried all four of the bags to the front door at once. My fingers were about to fall off, but I had told J.D. he didn't have to worry about anything, and that meant carrying groceries, too. I kept my promises.

I rang the bell, and J.D. ushered me inside. He was on the phone, FaceTiming someone. When he reached down to grab some of the bags from me, the screen of his phone faced me. I smiled at the older man looking back.

"Who's the pretty girl?" the man asked. "Date tonight?"

"No," J.D. said. "Grandpa, this is Charlie." He flashed the screen back toward me so I could wave.

"Pleasure to meet you, Charlie," his grandfather said. And then J.D. turned the phone back so his grandfather could see him. "Ahh," his grandfather continued, "that's the girl who—"

"Grandpa!" J.D.'s volume increased. "It's FaceTime, so she can still hear you, remember?"

I held back a laugh. *The girl who what?* I wondered. Wanted to date Teo? Gave J.D. a hard time for being late? Was a dictator at the paper? I took off my jacket and waited for them to finish their conversation.

His grandfather said, "That's right. I'll let you two sweethearts get back to what you were doing."

J.D. looked like he was trying not to cringe as he said his good-byes. Then he turned toward me and said, "Please don't read into that. He just gets confused sometimes."

It would have been so easy to give him a hard time about what just transpired, but something in his eyes told me it wasn't the time. "It's okay," I said instead. "Is that the grandfather who moved to Florida?"

He nodded. He got a faraway look for a moment, and then all of a sudden it was like he remembered I was there. His expression changed to mock outrage. "Where is your sweater?" he demanded. "I may have to kick you out. Rules are rules, and I know how seriously you take those."

"I do." I reached into one of the bags and pulled out my monstrosity of a garment and put it on. "That's why I have this." It was green, had the words *This girl loves Christmas* on it in red, along with two hands with the thumbs pointing at the wearer, aka me. Then to up the hideous holiday factor, there were Christmas trees, stockings, ornaments, and candy canes surrounding the words, all in the shape of a wreath.

J.D. laughed and clapped his hands together. "That is priceless. Where did you get that?"

I couldn't pretend I went out especially to buy it; I only found out about the party last night. "My mom gave it to me as a present," I admitted. "I saw it in a store a few years ago and laughed, and said it encapsulated my love for Christmas. I had been joking, but my mom thought I was serious, and thus I became the proud recipient of an ugly holiday sweater."

"Well, I may have you beat. I will be right back."

When he came back downstairs, it was my turn to laugh. J.D. did a full pirouette for me. On the front of the sweater was Rudolph, but it wasn't just a picture of him; it was actually protruding, like someone sewed a stuffed animal on it. And on the back of the sweater? Rudolph's hind legs and tail. Garland entwined the sleeves.

"I'll give it to you," I said. "As much as I hate coming in second, I think you win."

He hit his hand over his heart. "I don't know if I can take the shock. You willingly conceding first place?"

"Hey," I said. "I'm not delusional. I know there are things I will never be the best at. I'll never throw a football like Teo, get everyone in school to spill their secrets like Zakiyah, do math in my head the way Morgan does, or," I said, flicking Rudolph's nose, "pick out the most hideous holiday sweater in existence. I mean, how can I compete with that?"

"I know," he said. "But come on, did you really think I'd have an ugly Christmas sweater party if I didn't have one?"

"You bought that?"

"Nope," he said, moving the bags closer to the dining room table. "Back of my mom's closet. I told you she loves Christmas." Our mothers were never, ever, ever allowed to go shopping together.

"Let's see what you have here," J.D. said, and we started to pull things out of the bags. There were cups, plates, a punch bowl, ladle, napkins, chocolate, chips, soda, and, my favorite, eggnog. "*Three* cartons?" He held up one of the cartons. "We're six people. This is way too much."

"Speak for yourself," I said, taking it from him and pouring it into the punch bowl. "I can drink one of these on my own. I love eggnog, and I haven't had any this year."

"I'm not a fan of it," he said.

"What is wrong with you? It is like a Christmas milkshake." I added the second carton to the bowl.

Just then the bell rang. Maybe it was Teo. "You have to help me," I begged J.D. "Morgan and Ira are going to be in on it, but the more the better. I need you to keep Heather away from your cousin so I can get that Teo time we talked about before. Remember?"

"Like you'd let me forget your mission?" he said.

That was true. I smiled as he went to get the door. My plan was all coming together!

Twenty-Seven

Turned out it was Morgan and Ira at the door. They also came in without their ugly Hanukkah sweater. After about six attempts to figure out how to put their jackets on over their shared top and carry the baked goods that they were bringing, they had decided to wait until they got to J.D.'s.

"I can't believe how cold it is out there," Morgan said as she and Ira tried to put on their sweater. "It's a good thing you live next door, J.D. I would not have wanted to walk too far in this weather."

"I'm just glad last night's snow stuck!" I said. We wound up with about three inches, enough to make me happy.

"Well, what do you think?" Ira said once they finally got their ugly sweater on.

"I think you fit right in with the rest of us," J.D. said. We definitely weren't winning any fashion prizes. J.D. pulled his camera off the end table and snapped a few pictures. I was having such a great day that despite my ensemble I smiled for the photos anyway.

The doorbell rang again, and my heart sped up. It had to be Teo!

And it was. Only Heather was with him. Had they come together—like a date? No. They were friends, and Teo probably just gave her a ride. There was something between us this afternoon, I knew it. Still, looking at the two of them gave me pause.

Stop it, Charlie. No insecurities. No shyness. *Be bold.* I walked right over to him and gave him a hug. But it wasn't a good hug, he felt . . . bumpy.

"It's my sweater," he explained, taking off his long navy jacket to reveal his ugly holiday creation. A regular green sweater that he had attached round ornaments to. There were about ten of them splattered across his front, in a variety of colors.

"Nice," I said.

"It was my idea," Heather offered, revealing her own getup.

Instead of a sweater, she went with a sweater dress. And it wasn't ugly. It was tight and short and red. The only thing even remotely unusual about it was that she took Christmas lights and wrapped them around her waist as a belt. I kicked myself for not thinking to do the same. Once again, Heather looked adorable and I looked like someone's crazy grandma.

"I like your sweaters," Morgan said, and attempted to make her way over to them to say hello. She almost fell in the process. Seems she and Ira were still getting a handle on being attached. She had forgotten to tell him she was moving, so while she started walking, he kept still. She caught her balance just in time, and they both started laughing. "This way," she directed him, and they began walking in unison. "I'm Morgan," she said, introducing herself to Heather.

"And I'm Ira," her Siamese twin said.

We all did the pleasantries and then I gave J.D., Morgan, and Ira . . . the look. The keep-Heather-busy look.

"Uh, Heather," J.D. said, coming through for me, "can I, um, show you around?"

"Yeah, okay." She didn't look enthused. She didn't exactly want a house tour, but at least she said yes. As I watched them head for the kitchen, I realized I was beginning to like J.D. more and more. He was a good friend.

Morgan knew to give me space to be with Teo, so she and Ira waddled over to the couch and sat down.

"I love the key chain," he said to me. "I've already killed way too much time on it, and I haven't even had it a full day."

"I could take it back if it's causing you problems," I teased.

He winked at me. "I think I can handle it. I've been at the hospital a couple of times this week, but I haven't seen you."

He'd been looking for me?! "I haven't been there very much," I confessed. "My mom doesn't usually have a set break time, so I don't bother going. But it's not like I even see you in school that often," I said, hoping he would pick up the hint that he should look for me in the halls more! Honestly, we saw each other so infrequently, I was tempted to make him an honorary editor of the paper, just so he'd be at the *Sentinel* editorial meetings.

"Well, we'll have to change that." Score. He took the hint. "Want to grab a drink?"

"Yeah," I said. "I brought eggnog."

"Perfect." He patted his sweater. "I brought something, too. It will make this party more fun. Know what I mean?"

"I do," Heather said, appearing out of nowhere. J.D. lagged behind her.

I would have thought my eyes bugging out at him would have clued J.D. in to the fact that I needed him to pull Heather away again, but he just gave me one of those nothing-I-can-do-about-it shrugs.

Teo pulled out a little flask. "Rum," he said.

"Really, Teo?" J.D. said. "My mom has, like, three rules. Are you trying to break them all?"

"I don't know," he said. "There's the 'no groups over when she's not home,' 'no illegal activity,' and . . ." He dangled the flask. "What's the third?"

J.D. just scowled and walked over to Morgan and Ira and plopped himself in the recliner near them.

I got where J.D. was coming from; I was all about following the rules. I was actually kind of surprised Teo wasn't the same way. With a schedule like his, I would have thought he was extremely by the book.

"Who's in?"

"No, thanks," Morgan said. Ira shook his head no. And J.D. just sat there, silent.

I felt bad that he was upset; I knew I should have told Teo to put it away, but things were going so smoothly with us right now. I didn't want to look like I was all about J.D. and what he wanted. Besides, it wasn't like Teo was going to drive—he was spending the night at his cousin's, and he wasn't pressuring anyone to drink.

"Looks like it's just the three of us," he said.

"Two," I corrected him. "I'm just going to have the regular."

"Okay. Hey, J.D., peppermint extract?" Teo called out to him before turning his attention back to me. "You have to try it. With or without alcohol, it makes eggnog like Christmas in a cup." I already thought of it as a Christmas milkshake. This made it sound even better.

"Cabinet next to the stove," J.D. muttered.

"I'll get it," I volunteered.

When I came back, Teo said, "The left two have alcohol, right is regular. Just a little drop of the mint to each. Too much will overpower it." I carefully did as instructed. Not that Teo or Heather noticed. They were engrossed in a conversation about people I didn't know.

I took my cup and looked back at the crew on the couch for help.

"Heather," Morgan called out to her. "I want to hear more about the Aca-mazings. Come tell me everything. How long have you been doing it?"

Now that was a best friend. Heather grabbed her drink and went over to the couch, leaving me alone with Teo.

"Cheers," he said, picking up the third cup.

We clinked drinks, and I got one of those premonition feelings.

Today we were toasting with giant red plastic cups, and hopefully, pretty soon we'd be at Noelle's party together using real glasses. And maybe, if things went according to plan, we'd be clinking again on New Year's Eve leading right into my birthday.

I took a sip. Eggnog was hands down my favorite drink of all time. I wasn't sure what I thought about the mint. It certainly gave it a kick.

"Well?" Teo said.

"Delicious," I said. "Can't go wrong with eggnog."

I was a little nervous standing there. Could I just come right out and ask him to Noelle's? I chugged down half of my drink in record time. I wasn't ready to go there yet. I had to work my way up to that. Start slow. "I can't believe Christmas is almost here. What's your family doing?" I asked.

"Christmas Eve is at my house and then Christmas Day my family comes here. What about you?"

"This year it's low-key. In the past my mom and I hosted a huge Christmas Eve dinner, a bunch of close family friends and others came by, and then on Christmas morning it was just us. We would go to mass, open presents, eat a whole tray of spicy cinnamon rolls with cream cheese frosting, and watch holiday movies all day. This year, we have the shortened version because of her shifts at the hospital."

"She's stuck working on Christmas?" he asked.

"Yeah, but at least I have her for the morning. It's not so bad. And then, of course the next day is Noelle's Christmas Ball. I can't wait. Are you going?"

"Noelle's ball?" Heather jumped up from the couch. Had they all been sitting there just listening to me and Teo?

"Huh?" I asked.

"Sorry," she said, "it was hard not to hear. I want to go to that party so bad. I heard she's having Kevin Wayward play. Tickets for his last show sold out in minutes, and she has him playing her *birthday party*. It's insane. Noelle invited the whole junior class, but she said a handful of people still haven't RSVP'd, so she might invite some of us seniors. I really want to be one of them."

I was afraid to ask if she knew the theme was Lovers' Ball and that Noelle was pushing everyone to be a couple. The last thing I needed was for Heather to ask Teo before I did. Or worse, for me to ask him only to find out he wanted to see if Heather was going before he accepted any other invitation. I couldn't risk that. I had to make sure Teo was definitely into me before I invited him. I only had one shot, and I needed this date. Zakiyah would never let me live it down if I went solo.

"I really don't think the Kevin Wayward thing is true," I told her, hoping to sway her away from wanting to go. "I'm pretty sure Noelle would have told me."

"I heard it was supposed to be a surprise appearance," she said. "And even if there's just a slight chance, I don't care. I want to be there."

Before I could regain control of the conversation and steer it toward something Charlie-and-Teo-centric, Heather launched into a ten-minute monologue about how she loved fancy parties and went into how she was spending the holiday. That girl could talk and talk *and talk*, but I couldn't leave. The plan was not to give her and Teo time alone. So I just stood there and suffered, drinking my weight's worth in eggnog. I had polished off the entire cup, and Heather was still yammering away. I got in a few mm-hmms and yeahs, but that was about it. She had taken over and showed no sign of stopping.

I should have worn my comfortable boots. Instead I had gone for the stylish ones, to try and counterbalance the ugliness factor of the sweater, but I was regretting that now. My feet were hurting. I swayed back and forth, trying to alleviate the pressure from one foot onto the other. It was kind of relaxing, and dulled some of the Heather-speak that just went on and on.

Blah, blah, blah, Mr. Harmon's exam was so hard. . . . I heard Janelle left the room crying. . . . Reading assignments that will go right through vacation? Who does that? . . . The Aca-mazings have a really good shot at nationals this year. . . . Teo, we need you back on the team. . . . At the very least, come root us on. . . . I'm gonna watch Ferris Bueller's Day Off *tomorrow so you stop bugging me about it. . . . I'm going to pick one for you to watch, too. . . . I may have a New Year's party, still trying to convince my parents. . . . You'd come, right? . . . Should it be themed? . . . Polly thinks she's getting a car for graduation, did she tell you? . . . Reggie and Cory make the cutest couple. . . . I wonder if we'll get any snow days this year. . . .*

Ugh. Stop talking, stop talking, stop talking. I could not even listen anymore. My head was getting foggy from all her blathering.

I needed to sit, to shake off the dizziness from all the

nonsense she was spewing. I moved to one of the dining room chairs. "Ow," I cried out. I slightly misjudged where it was positioned and rammed my arm into it.

"Are you okay?" Morgan asked.

"I'm fine," I said, and then I sat down and crossed my arms over my chest.

"What's with you?"

She knew. I made a pouty face at her to drive the point home. She had failed at her job. She was supposed to keep Heather away, and she didn't.

Morgan stood up and then fell back to the couch. She forgot to tell Ira she was getting up and the sweater dragged her back. The look on her face! Then she pulled Ira by the arm, and they both made their way over to me.

They looked hysterical. "You two," I said, pointing, "are the funniest-looking people ever." I couldn't stop laughing. I don't know why, but it just hit me how ridiculous it was that they were attached.

"Are you drunk?" Morgan asked.

"Just on Christmas," I said.

"And possibly rum?" she offered.

"Nope, I had the regular stuff," I told her.

"Actually," Heather said, "I drank my whole cup, and I don't feel anything. Did you pick up mine by mistake?"

"The right was regular, and that's what I took." I wasn't drunk. I'd know if I was, wouldn't I? I moved my head back and forth. It felt as if there were a magnetic force helping move it, making it

196

feel extra heavy. But that was probably just because I was over-thinking it.

"Oh no," Teo said.

"What?" J.D. asked. He didn't sound happy.

"The way the drinks were set and how we were standing, my right would have been her left. I didn't even think about it."

J.D. ran his hands through his hair. He looked stressed.

"It's okay," I assured him.

"No, it's not," Morgan answered instead.

She was making such a big deal out of nothing—and in front of Teo! "It's not like I never drank anything before."

She gave a giant eye roll. "Two sips of champagne at a wedding doesn't count."

I stuck my tongue out at her. She could be so difficult when she wanted to be.

Morgan turned to Teo like I wasn't even there. "Now she's had how much?"

"A lot," he said. "I gave a *very, very* generous pour."

"Okay," J.D. said. "Come on, Charlie." He sat me on the couch. "I think it's time for this party to be over."

"No!" I objected, but no one was listening to me, which I found very rude. This was supposed to be a party. Why was everyone sooo serious?

Morgan pulled the sweater off of her and Ira. She was right, it was hot in here. I needed to get rid of my sweater, too. But the stupid, ugly thing kept getting all caught, and I couldn't get it off. I tugged at the sleeve.

Morgan moved closer and put one hand on each side of me. "Are you okay?"

She looked so intense. She needed to lighten up. I reached up and poked her nose with my finger. "Are *you* okay?"

"You are drunk."

"No, I'm not."

"Yeah, you are," Teo said, laughing.

"This is not funny," Morgan hissed at him.

I didn't know you could hiss that word. There wasn't an *s* in it. "Funny," I repeated. She was much better at it than I was. "Funnneee," I practiced again. "Funnneeee."

"Give me your keys and your phone," Morgan said.

"Why?"

She looked annoyed to have to explain, but I wasn't the one asking to take her stuff. She wanted mine! I deserved an explanation.

"Because you can't go home like this," she said. "And we can't go to my house, either. So I'm just going to text your mom that you are staying with me, and tell my parents that I'm staying with you. And then we have to move your car, so my parents don't see it and get suspicious."

Huh? She was using a lot of words now. But I had to prove to her that I was perfectly fine. So I just bobbed my head in agreement and handed her my stuff.

"I'll move her car," Ira offered.

"Teo was supposed to give me a ride home," Heather said.

"I'll do it," Ira said.

"Go, Ira!" I cheered. He was getting rid of my competition.

Finally, one of them was coming through. Morgan shook her head at me.

"Good night, everyone," Ira said.

I stood up. "Wait, you're not coming back?" I wanted Heather gone, not him.

"The party is over," J.D. said again.

"Why?"

"Because you're drunk," J.D. and Ira said at the same time. *Did they rehearse that?*

"Charlie, why don't you lie down," Morgan said, trying to get me back to the couch.

"Because it's a party!" There were still four of us there—including Teo. This was my time to impress him. "You don't sleep at parties," I said, breaking away from Morgan's grasp. I was free. The room was spinning toward the left, so I put out my arms and starting twirling toward the right.

"Come on, do it with me!" I instructed them all.

"Oh God," J.D. said.

What was wrong with him? He was always telling me to lighten up, but here he was being the boring one.

I looked over at Teo. He was staring at me and smiling. I waved. *Ha-ha, Heather, I'm the one he's focused on.*

J.D. really knew how to throw a party, and I knew just what I wanted to do next.

Twenty-Eight

"What kind of party doesn't have dancing?" I asked. "Come on, Teo." I took his hands and began to twirl around.

I gave him my sultriest look. I'm pretty sure he gave one back, although it could have been my imagination coupled with wishful thinking. Damn all those TV movies Morgan made me sit through.

"I can't watch this," J.D. said. "I'm going to clean up."

"I'll help," Morgan told him. She turned to Teo. "Are you drunk?"

"Just a slight buzz."

"Make sure she doesn't do anything stupid," she warned him.

I rolled my eyes at her. Like I ever did anything stupid. I continued to dance. "Dip me," I instructed Teo, and then fell back in his arms.

"Whoa," he said, "careful there." Then he lifted me back to a standing position, but I preferred his arms, so I let myself fall back again. It was like a seesaw. Standing, Teo, standing, Teo. *I could do this all night.* Although it wasn't meant to be.

"Let's sit for a minute," Teo said.

I conceded.

It was strange. The whole room circled really fast when my eyes were closed, and was back to normal when they were open. There had to be a scientific explanation for that; I'd have to investigate in the morning.

"I'll be right back," Teo told me.

I let out a sigh after he left. This party was getting pretty boring. *Wait. Where was J.D.?* I hadn't seen him in a while. Had he left? But it was his house. I had to go check.

I grabbed my coat and went outside. I took a deep breath. It smelled like winter, like Christmas. I loved it. I kicked some snow with the top of my boot. J.D.'s lawn had a beautiful blanket of snow, only a few footprints. I wondered if they were J.D.'s. Maybe I needed to follow them.

I placed one foot onto one footprint, and then took a really long step to match up with the next one.

"Found her," Morgan shouted. "What are you doing?"

"Looking for J.D.," I said.

"Charlie, come inside. He's there."

"Make him come out here," I told her.

"No, you need to come in before my parents see you."

"Hi, Mr. and Mrs. Levine," I called out.

"Charlie!"

Before I could ask her what she was yelling about, J.D. was

making his way over to me. "J.D.," I said, giving him a big hug. "I thought I lost you. Come make angels with me." I threw myself back into the snow and started wiping my arms up and down. I hoped we'd have some more snow for Christmas.

"Let's get you up," he said, and leaned down to lift me.

But I didn't want to go inside, so I wrapped my arms around his waist and pulled him down. He fell right on top of me. He quickly scrambled off, and I couldn't help but laugh at the look of surprise on his face. "We need to go inside," he said.

"One angel first," I begged.

"Okay," he said, "one angel."

Our bodies together captured in the snow. I wondered if there was a way to save it? A frozen J.D. and Charlie snow angel for posterity. Maybe if I shoveled it out carefully and found a big freezer.

"There," Morgan butted in. "You have your angel. Can we all go in now?"

"Nope," I said and got up and ran. I picked up a snowball and threw it at J.D. "Got you!"

I waited for him to make his move. Was he going to go left? Right? I would be ready.

"Charlie," he said, and I ran for it.

I took a left and hid behind the tree. When I peeked out, he grabbed me and picked me up over his shoulder. "You're really strong," I said.

"And you're really drunk."

"Why does everyone keep . . ." All of a sudden, my stomach started to churn. "Put me down, put me down, put me down."

He did and then it happened so fast. My mac and cheese dinner, the eggnog, and whatever else was in my stomach lurched out of me. Oh no, oh no. *Please tell me I didn't get his shoes, please tell me I didn't get his shoes.*

If I did, he didn't say anything. He just moved behind me. With one hand he held back my hair, and he placed the other on my back. "You're okay, you're okay."

I wanted to tell him to leave, to get Morgan over. But I couldn't. She was a sympathetic puker. If she saw someone barf, half the time she would, too.

After a minute, when it seemed the wave had passed, he said, "Let's get you inside." He picked me back up, and I rested my head on his shoulder. J.D. was so nice.

The next thing I remembered, I woke up with my body hunched over near the toilet and my head resting on the seat.

"Are you okay?" someone asked, stirring to life from the bathtub.

"J.D.?"

"Do you need water, or—?"

I couldn't answer. I turned back to the toilet and threw up.

When I woke up the next time, I was on the couch. Morgan was on the love seat kitty-corner from me. And J.D. was in the recliner. There was a blanket over me. He must have tucked me in.

My head was still spinning, I felt like crap, and I could barely see straight, but I closed my eyes and smiled. Morgan had been right about J.D. all along. He really was a good person. It was the last thing I thought about before I fell asleep.

Twenty-Nine

My head was throbbing when I woke up the next morning, and the light shining through the window hurt my eyes.

I rubbed my temples, trying to put together the pieces of the night before. Little snippets came flashing back. Trying to dance with Teo and forcing him to dip me a dozen times, making snow angels outside and . . . oh no, no, no, no, no, no—did I throw up on J.D.? He had been nice about it. He tucked me in. Still . . .

How could I let myself get so out of control?

Where was everybody? I got up, and a shooting pain pulsed through my head. I was never drinking again. Not that this time was by choice.

I followed the voices coming from the kitchen.

"She rises," J.D. said.

"What time is it?"

"Ten," Morgan said. "Do you want something to eat?"

My mouth twisted at the thought. The last thing I wanted was food.

"I am so sorry about last night, I don't—"

"Stop," J.D. said. "It wasn't your fault. Teo did this. He shouldn't have brought the alcohol to begin with."

"So what do you remember?" Morgan asked. "Taking the wrong cup and getting totally wasted?"

I nodded.

"And how about when Teo got up to go to the bathroom, and you wandered outside?"

"Yeah, unfortunately, I remember that, too. . . . I'm so sorry. For everything." What could I say? It was bad enough Morgan saw me like that, but I didn't even want to look at J.D. How embarrassing! *I puked on his shoes.* At least I was fairly sure I did, and then he got me back in the house, held my hair as I threw up all night, and I think he even slept in the bathtub to make sure I was okay.

"I told you, it's not your fault," J.D. said.

"Don't be mad at Teo. I was the one who took the wrong cup."

Instead of responding, he just gave me an ibuprofen and a glass of water. "Take this," he said.

I looked at the pill and did as advised. Anything to get rid of the banging inside my head. It was a good thing I still had tomorrow to do my homework; there was no way I'd be able to think straight today. "Thank you. Where is everybody else?" Then something came back to me. "Wait, did Ira take my car?"

"Yep. He drove Heather home, moved your car, then got his and went home so his parents wouldn't flip out."

"Where's my car?"

"Down the street," she said. "In the back parking lot of Sand-brook Elementary. I couldn't risk my parents seeing it around here. They thought I was with you."

"Hey," Teo said, joining us.

I jumped up. "Teo, I am so embarrassed."

"No, I should be. I'm sorry," he said. "It's my fault you got drunk and wandered outside. I was just gone for a minute. I wanted to help bring you back in, but . . ."

His voice trailed off, and Morgan filled in the rest. "I told him he'd done enough."

That seemed like something she'd say.

Morgan stood up. "As much fun as the past fourteen hours have been, I've got to go. I have to make ten dozen cookies for the elementary school PTA parent helpers."

"That's kind of a disappointing gift," Teo said, grabbing an apple from the fridge. "What? They each get one cookie?" Why was he egging her on? Especially after what just happened. I needed my best friend to like my hopefully-someday-future boyfriend.

"No," Morgan said, her voice straining to stay calm. "They each get their own dozen."

"That makes no sense," he said.

"What are you talking about?" I asked. My head hurt too much to try and sort out what he was saying.

He leaned back against the fridge. "There has to be more than ten parent helpers. There are three elementary schools in town."

Morgan's face turned ashen. "He's right. Each grade has three classes, each class has one or two primary parent helpers. And multiply that by three. That's about a hundred." She turned to me. "Please tell me it's just for the PTA heads or something."

I reached for my pocket. "Do any of you guys happen to have my phone?" Morgan handed it to me. I punched up my albums. I had taken a picture of the order. I always did that as an extra precaution. I breathed a sigh of relief. "It says ten, see?" I held the phone out to them.

Morgan fell back into her chair. "No, it doesn't, Charlie. That says *a hundred and ten*."

"No," I said, turning the screen back to me. I did *not* make mistakes like that. But I had. The second *1* on the order was so close to the first that I just thought Ms. Tashy had traced over it to make sure it was visible. How could I have done this? My mom was a doctor; I was used to messy writing. I had screwed up royally.

Talk about sobering up quickly. Fear and adrenaline rushed through my body. "Are we going to be okay?" I asked Morgan.

"No," she said. "They have to be delivered Monday morning, and I have to have everything done by tonight. Tomorrow is out. The afternoon is the Hebrew School Hanukkah party, and I'm making the doughnuts, cupcakes, and cookies fresh in the morning. Plus, my parents are having our annual latke night that evening. They'll need the kitchen. I'm going to be booted."

"We can just work all night tonight," I assured her.

"Like my parents will let that happen. If I'm in there too late, they'll make me stop."

"How long will it take to get everything done?"

She started throwing out some numbers. "Twelve cookies to a tray, two shelves, a ten-minute cook time. If we get one tray in immediately after we take one out, and decorate the gingerbread men and box everything up while two batches are baking, we're still looking at more than nine hours—and that's not including the initial prep or getting all the ingredients, extra ribbon, and boxes. We're dead."

"Can't you just cut down on the number of cookies in each box?" Teo asked.

"No," she answered. "We told them it would be a dozen. Six chocolate chip, five peanut butter blossoms, and one gingerbread man."

"Cut the price in half; I'm sure it'll be fine," Teo said. "It's better than not giving them anything."

"That will make us look horrible." I understood that not delivering was even worse, but I didn't want to do a mediocre job. And we couldn't afford to mess this up. We already were pretty much foregoing any profit. We cut the PTA a really awesome deal because we thought it would be a way in the door. No wonder they ordered so many. We weren't that much more than a box of Chips Ahoy! but homemade, and in a much prettier package.

"I'll do whatever I can," I said.

"You have a hangover, and you can barely bake on a good day."

Ouch. But it was true.

"I'm sure Ira will help," I told her.

"I will, too," J.D. said. "And we can use the oven here. It will cut the time in half."

A little bit of color returned to her cheeks. "Maybe this can work."

"It has to," I said.

"I'd help you guys if I could," Teo added, "but I'm due at the hospital in a half hour. And then I have to meet Reggie. I promised him the other day. And finish my history paper."

I couldn't be mad at him for volunteering. Or, truth be told, even for meeting his friend or doing his paper. He had plans; he shouldn't have had to cancel them because of something I did. Besides, this was my mess to clean up, not his.

"You can get this done," he said, moving toward me and squeezing my shoulder. "I have faith in you. I'm sorry, but I do have to get out of here. I don't want to be late."

I loved that he was a planner, super motivated, scheduled, and constantly busy, but as I watched him walk off, a small part of me kind of wished he wasn't.

Thirty

I always thought I was the organized one, but Morgan had the cookie-making assembly line down to an exact science. While Ira was out picking up the extra supplies, under Morgan's strict tutelage, we started making dough with the ingredients we already had in her kitchen. Once we had that finished, Morgan sent J.D. and me to his house to use his oven, and instructed one of us to return when we needed more dough, that she would have it ready. J.D. and I were in charge of the peanut butter blossoms, basically peanut butter cookies with a Hershey's kiss in the center. Once we hit 110 dozen, then we would help with the chocolate chip cookies and the packaging. Morgan didn't trust me to decorate the gingerbread men. Not that I blamed her. (The gingerbread house my mother and I decorated looked more like a house of horrors.)

J.D. pulled out trays nine and ten, and I handed him eleven

and twelve. We quickly put the chocolate kiss in the middle of each cookie and moved them onto a plate to cool so we could start loading the next batches.

"I think we can probably fit more than twelve on each tray," I said as we rolled the dough into little balls.

"I'm not messing with Morgan's system," he said. "She seems to know what she's doing."

"True." I didn't know what to say after that. We had only made small talk since we started baking, skirting the real issue—what he had done for me. Yet for some reason it felt odd bringing it up. I just felt awkward around him. He had seen, heard, *smelled,* way too much. We went back to silence.

After a couple more batches, J.D. held up a little round ball of dough. "This is your brain," he said, putting on an extra-deep voice. Then he squashed it. "This is your brain on alcohol."

"What?" I asked.

"It's an old PSA that I saw online, only they used an egg, and I think it was drugs not alcohol."

"My head does kind of feel like that," I agreed.

"Okay." He dropped the dough back into the bowl. "That was supposed to lighten the mood. I'm used to angry Charlie, thinks-she's-always-right Charlie, funny Charlie, Christmas-loving Charlie, and any of those Charlies I have an idea how to talk to. Timid-silent Charlie? I don't know this girl."

"It's just—" I stopped and went to go check on the latest batch of cookies.

"What?"

I was still facing the stove. "I was a mess last night. I danced

211

around, I threw myself in the snow, refused to go inside, got sick, and your *shoes* . . ." I cringed just thinking about it again.

"You missed them, if it's any consolation," he said.

It wasn't.

The night played back in my head, everything J.D. had done for me. I turned back to face him. "Why did you do all that for me?"

His face got serious. "You needed help. I didn't want to see you get hurt. You're my friend."

I felt my eyes tear up. "But I haven't exactly been the greatest to you."

"I think we've come a long way, and besides," he said, leaning into me conspiratorially, "here's a secret. I never really hated you. Sure, you annoyed me. A lot. But Morgan was always going on and on about how great you were, so I figured there had to be something there."

We locked eyes. I didn't know how to respond to that. He had really been there for me. "Thank you for everything," I said. He deserved a lot more than that; I just didn't have the words.

He nodded. We stayed there holding each other's gaze a moment longer. He finally broke it. "Um, I should go get some more dough from Morgan," he said.

"Yeah," I agreed.

When he returned, the mood had lightened.

"Now, you know," he said, "I can probably come up with some great superhero names for you after last night."

I covered my face with my arm. "Please no," I said, but that just nudged him forward.

"The Eggnog Avenger," he declared. "She'll spew holiday spirit at the first sign of trouble."

I groaned. "That's really bad."

"How about this one then? The Holiday Hell-raiser—she'll raise a lot more than trouble."

"Stick to the photography," I told him.

"You think it's so easy, you try it."

"My brain is still so scrambled, I can't think straight right now," I said.

His face got serious. "Do you want to lie down? I can finish this on my own."

My head was throbbing, the backs of my eyes were burning, and I wanted to go back to sleep so bad, but there was no way I was not finishing these cookies.

"I got this," I said.

"You sure?" he asked. "Because it's really okay if you want to go to bed. I can do it."

I shook my head. "No, this is a job for the Buzzed Baker—she can party all night and raise the dough in the morning."

"And you thought mine were bad?" he asked, and we both started laughing.

For someone who prided herself on her attention to detail, I had really been off my game recently. First the PTA order, and now J.D.

I had been so wrong about him. He truly was an incredible guy.

Thirty-One

When we finally finished the cookies, I went home and slept and slept and slept. Sunday morning, I felt so much better. I helped Morgan and Ira deliver and set everything up for the Hebrew School Hanukkah party, and then I rushed back to my house. I had work to do. I had already gotten Morgan a gift, but after yesterday, she deserved more. And I definitely needed something for J.D., too. I finished with their presents right in time to head to Morgan's.

"Hey," she said, opening the door for me. She was all smiles. I could understand why. Her house was filled with energy and delicious smells. Her dad and uncle were in the kitchen frying up some latkes with several hungry takers waiting for the latest batch. Ira and one of Morgan's cousins were playing a car-racing video game, with her brother backseat driving from behind the couch. And her mom and the rest of the family (grandparents, more uncles, aunts, and cousins) were all laughing, eating, and telling stories. I always loved coming here when her whole— as her grandma called it—*mishpachah* was there. It was the Yiddish word for family. It was like you could almost feel the love. My mom and I had the love part, too, but we were missing the large crowd. I wasn't complaining; I wouldn't trade what I had with my mom for anything, but there was something really nice about seeing a whole big family together.

After I had more than my fair share of potato pancakes (I was so glad my stomach was better) with huge dollops of applesauce and sour cream, her family lit the Hanukkah menorah and sang songs. I knew a bunch of them and jumped right in. And this time, I wasn't the only one with a non-Aca-mazing voice. Then it was present time. Morgan's parents even got me something—a beautiful gold necklace with my birthstone, and Morgan had gotten me the matching earrings. She had similar ones that I was always complimenting.

I pulled her aside to give her my gift. "You are such an amazing friend," I said. "Thank you for yesterday, thank you for everything." I handed her the first gift. I had put it together more than a month ago. She ripped off the paper. "A recipe book!" Then her eyes widened, she flipped through the pages, and tears started rolling down her cheeks. "Charlie, you didn't!" It wasn't just any recipe book; it was her recipes. I had used one of those online photo services and created a hardcover book. I typed in all of her recipes and accompanied them with pictures of her food that I stole from her GroupIt page. J.D. had taken a bunch of the photos for her, and they looked pretty professional.

"Don't cry," I said. "You'll make me cry."

"It's just that this is the most thoughtful gift anyone has ever given me."

"You deserve it," I said. I more than meant it. "And there's this," I said, smiling. "You earned this, too, especially with everything lately."

She opened the envelope I gave her and started laughing. It was a lifetime get-out-of-lateness-free pass.

"Now don't take advantage of it," I told her.

"I wouldn't dream of it," she said, and pulled me into a big hug. And I knew she wouldn't. Because I really did have the best friend in the whole world.

My gift giving was far from over. I decided to give Teo his fourth Secret Santa present Monday at school, but my faith in the plan was starting to waver. Maybe I had been imagining all the moments between Teo and me. He never even called or texted to see if I met the cookie deadline or how I was feeling. How hard would a *hope you're doing okay* text have been?

I went straight to my locker when I got to school. As I was storing my books and Teo's gift, I felt something lightly touch my shoulder, and I quickly turned around.

It was Teo.

"Hi," he said.

"Hi," I answered, unsure of what else to say.

"I was waiting for you to get here," he said.

"You were?"

He kicked a scuff mark on the ground. The always cool,

confident Teo looked uncomfortable. "Yeah, I wanted to apologize again. I'm really sorry. I'm really embarrassed. The whole night was my fault."

He was embarrassed? I was the one who made a fool of herself. "No it wasn't."

"Yeah it was. If you don't believe me, ask my cousin."

I smiled at him. "He'll forgive you."

"I know. But I'm more worried whether you will." He reached into his bag and pulled out a little box. "Maybe this will help make up for everything?" He handed it to me. "Open it."

I ripped off the wrapping paper and took off the top. There were a bunch of bangles inside.

"Five golden rings," he said. "I liked watching you out there singing. You were brave. I like that. This is a little reminder of that night."

"This is so sweet. Thank you." I looked up at him and smiled. "Maybe I can let everything about the weekend slide, just this once." Those doubts I had earlier were starting to melt.

"No, thank *you*," he said, and gave me a kiss on the cheek. When he did, his body lightly pressed up against mine.

I felt those little electric bolts run through me. He really was so sexy. He may have messed up, but he was coming through in the end. If we actually started dating, he'd be there for me, like now. We'd make plans together. We'd be a power couple. There was so much we could take on as a team.

"I have something for you, too," I said. I turned, reached into my locker for the baseball card, and presented it to him.

"You didn't have to get me anything else," he said.

"I wanted to."

"Charlie!" he said after he opened it. "I love it. This is incredible. It looks just like an official rookie card. Seriously, you are the world's best gift giver." That was an accolade that really belonged to J.D., but I bit my tongue.

"You're one to talk," I said instead. "You've been pretty spot-on yourself. Except for maybe that broken candy cane in the beginning. The rest, though?" I gave him the A-OK sign.

"I guess that's just one more thing we have in common," he said playfully.

"I guess so," I responded, matching his tone. Everything was back on track for us. I kicked myself for ever doubting him. Teo was the one for me, and after J.D. helped me find him the perfect gift for the *Sentinel* party, I was going to complete Operation Secret Santa by asking Teo to Noelle's party. There was no way we weren't going to that ball together. It was happening. I'd never been more sure of anything in my life.

Thirty-Two

"Ready?" J.D. asked me after school on Wednesday. I had been waiting by my car for eight minutes.

"I've been ready since the bell rang." Some things never changed. I should have known he'd be late.

"Sorry, I got here as soon as I could."

I took a deep breath. It was okay. After everything he had done for me, I could let this go. Instead of making a snide comment, I just got in the car.

"Where are we going?" I asked. The only information he had given me so far was a text that said bring boots and a baseball.

"It's a surprise."

Was he trying to push all of my buttons? "How am I supposed to drive there if I don't know where *there* is?"

"I will direct you, your own personal GPS."

I would have preferred the one on my phone.

"Did you bring the ball?" he asked. I pointed to the glove compartment. He took it out, threw it slightly up in the air, and caught it.

"And I need that for . . ."

"Can't tell you." He was so strange. What was he going to do? Make me paint it, doodle on it the way he did with his history notebook, print out Teo's photo on it?

"Okay," he said. "Take a right when we exit the parking lot."

"Just give me the address."

"Just try enjoying a little adventure."

There was no use objecting. He wasn't going to tell me, and I needed a final gift for Teo, so I took the right. And then I kept driving as he led me up one winding road and another until we were in the middle of nowhere.

"Okay, see that little dirt road up ahead?" he asked.

"Yeah."

"Take it." This did not seem like a smart idea; we were already on an out-of-the-way road. Who knew where this one would bring us?

"I don't think we're supposed to drive on it."

"It's a road," he said.

"An unpaved, uphill one."

He laughed. "The snow's been cleared. Just do it. We'll be fine. Park at the end of the road."

Against my better judgment, I did as instructed. He got out of the car, and I followed.

"This way," he said, pointing to a wooded area up ahead. An area with no walkway and covered in snow.

220

"Uh-uh. It's all snowy."

"And that's why I texted you last night to wear your boots. Come on."

He started walking, and I followed him. This was ridiculous. "What kind of gift am I going to find for Teo out here? Some branches? A jar of snow? Animal droppings?"

"Just wait. We're not here for Teo."

Then why were we there? I kept my eyes trained on the ground, watching as my footprints crunched in the snow. Other than the ones J.D. was making, and a couple of little animal prints, mine were the only ones out there.

"Have a seat," J.D. said, and wiped some snow off a big rock.

"It's wet."

"Fine, then just take a look around."

Whatever. The quicker I did it, the quicker I got to get out of there. I looked up and was totally stunned.

"Oh my God. It's gorgeous."

We were on the top of a hill that overlooked the center of town. It was like looking into a life-size snow globe. The First Congregational Church with its giant Christmas tree out in front looked like it could have been straight out of an old painting.

"This is my favorite spot," he said. He had his camera out and was snapping pictures. "I come here all the time to draw or write or just think. It's always my favorite right after it snows. Or in the fall once the leaves have changed colors."

It really was stunning. "How did you ever find this place?"

"Sometimes when my parents let me have the car, I go exploring."

"You just drive?" That seemed so random.

"Yes. Not everything has to be planned, Charlie, and sometimes you find something or somewhere you don't expect." He laughed. "Don't make that face. I found this place."

That was true.

"Come here, I want to show you something." He turned his camera so I could see one of the photos he took. It was of the whole scene—the church, the Christmas tree, the town. It was beautiful. Then he pulled up a different shot. It was a little icicle melting off of a small branch. It was equally as breathtaking.

"Those are really good."

He shrugged. "Thanks, and I know you have issues with some of the photos I take for the paper, but—"

"It's not issues."

"It's issues," he said.

"Okay, fine, I get in my mind what I want, and it's hard for me to change that."

He smiled. "I know. But sometimes it's good to challenge your thinking. The scene of the town makes a great photo, no question. But there are a lot of other things that do, too. And sometimes it's the smaller, not-as-in-the-center-of-it-all, less obvious choice that's the better one. The one that will surprise you."

"Maybe," I said.

"There's no maybe about it."

He was looking right at me, his expression so intense that I started to wonder if it was really photos he was talking about.

I looked back at him. "No?"

"No," he said.

"But how do you know?" I asked.

"It's a feeling. You go with your gut, not your head." His eyes were still on mine. "You have to trust your instincts."

We just stood there for a moment. Silent. Not moving. Then he leaned in slightly, and my breathing picked up. What was going on?

Oh. My. God.

Was J.D. Ortiz about to kiss me?

I was pretty sure he was.

As the thought crossed my mind, I let out a small gasp.

And just like that, the moment was over.

J.D. looked away, and I did, too.

"We should go," he said, turning from me. "We have a gift to get."

I followed him back to my car.

J.D. was back to his light, breezy self, as if he didn't just almost kiss me.

Probably because he didn't. I was being ridiculous.

Of course it was photos he was referring to. I don't even know why I would think anything else. J.D. didn't like me. Not like *that*. And that was a good thing, because I didn't think of him that way, either. We were friends. Nothing more.

So why couldn't I get what just happened out of my mind?

Thirty-Three

J.D. and I had barely spoken since we'd gotten back in the car. I didn't know what to say. J.D. seemed normal, but my mind was all over the place. I needed to snap out of it. He wasn't acting awkward or uncomfortable, so I wasn't going to, either. "We've been on this road forever. How much longer?" I asked, breaking the silence.

"We're getting there."

"If you're making me drive into New York," I told him, "just know that not only will I kill you, but my mom will, too."

"We're not going that far. Close, but not quite."

Twenty minutes later we pulled into a parking lot.

"You have got to be kidding me," I said, getting out of the car. "You made me drive over an hour to go to a pub?"

"Not just any pub," he said, tossing that stupid baseball again. "A pub owned in part by Manny Franco."

"Who?"

"Teo's favorite ballplayer."

Right. He had told me that. "So what are you going to do, bring him back a napkin? Taking *him* here would have been a nice surprise. Telling him *I* had a burger at his favorite player's sports bar, not so much."

"That's why we're going to do a lot better than that." He threw me the ball. "Like getting our own Manny autograph."

"Wait, what? He's here? Now? That's amazing!"

J.D. bobbed his head back and forth. "There is a chance he's here. I don't know for sure."

I was having a hard time grasping this. He made me come all the way up here for a maybe? "What do you mean, you're not sure?"

"Since Operation Secret Santa started, I've kept my eyes open for mentions of Manny sightings here," he said. "And it looks like he just got back to Connecticut last week. I called to ask if he'd be here. They wouldn't tell me for sure, but they said he's been here almost every night."

"*Almost.* What if he's not? The party is Friday. I won't have a gift for Teo."

"I'll sign the ball. I bet I could forge Manny's signature."

"J.D.!"

He laughed as he opened the door to the pub. "I'm kidding. If he's not, we'll figure something out. I'll come up with something."

"Are you forgetting you also have to turn in your photo spread tonight?" I asked.

"Hi," the hostess said before he could answer. "Just the two of you?"

"Yes, thank you." The place looked pretty empty, but I had to ask. "Any chance Manny is here?"

"Sorry, he's not," she answered as she led us to our table.

J.D. was a dead man. "Do you think he'll stop by later?" I asked.

"He could," she said, handing us each a menu. "Can I start you guys off with a drink?"

"I'll just have a water," I said.

"Coke, please," J.D. added.

"Be right back to take your order."

"Sounds good," J.D. replied.

He seemed pretty nonchalant for a guy whose whole plan was a bust. "What are we going to do?"

He picked up his menu. "It's still early. Let's give it some time."

I felt like my skin was curdling. Give it time? That was not a backup plan. "And what about the *Sentinel*?"

"What about it?"

"I told you it's due tonight. If you don't get your stuff in, we can't print on time, and the issue doesn't go out on Friday."

"What? The deadline's tonight? I thought I had another week."

"J.D., how could you do this?" I gripped the table. "I knew I never should have let you take charge. This is a disaster. What?" He had a stupid grin on his face. "Why are you smiling?"

He didn't answer, and it hit me. He was messing with me. I threw my napkin at him. "You are not funny."

"Did you really think I'd forget the deadline? You only told me and texted me about it just shy of a dozen times and had Morgan on my back for the past week. How scatterbrained do you think I am? I don't want you to answer that."

"So you have it done?"

"I just needed one more picture, and I got it today. It will be turned in as soon as I get home."

"Good," I said. "Do you have the proofs on your phone? Can I see them?"

"You can see it with everyone else. It's a surprise."

"I'm not everyone else, I'm the editor."

"Sorry," he said.

We had come so far, and yet he still managed to infuriate me.

I studied my menu. I was not in the mood to talk to J.D.

"Oh, come on," he said. "I promise you, it will meet your standards."

"My standards are very high."

"No kidding."

"Fine," I relented. He was a good photographer, I knew that, and despite our issues in the past, J.D. proved over the past few weeks that he could come through in a pinch. "I won't bring it up again. Just get it in on time. And make sure you get to the party on time, too."

"You want *me* at your party?"

I played with the edge of my napkin. "Yeah, you and Morgan are my only real friends on the paper, so yes, I want to make sure you show up."

That's right, I said it, to his face. J.D. was my friend. He had said it before, but I never said it back. I expected him to give me a hard time about it, but he just smiled. "I'll be there. I promise."

Over the next hour and a half while we chatted, the waitress took our order, brought our food, cleared our plates, and brought us the dessert menu, but there was still no sign of Manny.

"I'm thinking the peppermint chocolate molten lava cake," he said. "What about you?"

"I'm thinking I'm screwed for Friday. Let's just get out of here."

"But then you won't get your autograph."

I slunk down in the booth. "I'm not getting it anyway."

"Well, the least you can do is ask him before claiming defeat."

"What?"

He pointed to the bar. An older man was sitting there reading the paper.

I looked from the man to J.D. "That's Manny and you didn't tell me? He's been there for at least fifteen minutes; why didn't you say anything?"

"I thought you knew. You saw his baseball card at the store."

"Yeah, and he was, like, twenty years younger in it," I whispered. "There was no way I'd recognize him. If I did, I would have already been up there."

What was wrong with him? Manny was the whole reason we were having dinner at the pub.

"It wasn't like he was going anywhere. We were talking. I thought you could go up before we left."

Did he not know me at all? I did not wait for things. You had to do them when you had the chance. What if Manny got called away? Or started talking to someone? You had to strike when you saw an opportunity.

I took the baseball and went up to him. "Mr. Franco, sir?" I asked.

He looked over the newspaper at me.

"Yes?"

"I was wondering if you could sign this for me?" I held out the baseball. He didn't reach for it or even respond, so I just kept talking. "It's for this guy I really like. I know he'll go crazy over it."

"Your boyfriend over there?" he asked.

"No, that guy is *not* my boyfriend."

"Really? He keeps looking over at you, and the two of you seemed pretty caught up in each other when I walked in," Manny said, taking the ball from me and nodding in J.D.'s direction.

"I assure you there is nothing between us."

"Not how it looked to me, but if you say so," he said, a smirk on his face. "Who do ya want me to make this out to?"

"Teo, T-e-o." That was who I wanted. Not J.D.

He handed back the autographed baseball, and after thanking him profusely, I walked back over to the table.

"How did it go?"

I held up the signed ball so he could see. "Teo is going to freak out. This is definitely going to win him over. Thank you so much."

"Sure," he said, and then he leaned in and whispered, "I think Manny is staring at us."

"Ugh." I rolled my eyes. "Don't even ask. He thought we were dating."

"Us?" His eyebrows scrunched together.

"Yeah, crazy, right?"

"Totally," he said and scoffed. "Like that would ever happen." Then he gave one of those skeeved-out looks to drive the point home.

Seriously. The two of us only started tolerating each other recently. Dating was preposterous.

Yet the whole ride back to Sandbrook, Manny's words were all I could think about. *The two of you seemed pretty caught up in each other.* What a joke. I did not like J.D. Sure, he had done some nice things for me and was actually really funny when you got to know him, not to mention cute. But he also drove me crazy. *And* he laughed at the idea of us together.

Of course he did. We made no sense. We were way too different. Teo was the one for me. He was the smart choice. We both cared about grades and academic accolades and awards. We were planners. J.D. was all over the place. I didn't need spontaneity, I needed reliability. And that was Teo. He had a clear path ahead of him. He was an overachiever, we fit together. I couldn't even believe I was questioning it. Teo and I were clearly meant to be. Besides, it wasn't like J.D. liked me anyway.

Manny Franco needed to stick to baseball and running his restaurant, because he knew absolutely nothing about matchmaking.

I snuck a peek at J.D., and he was looking right back at me. I immediately put my eyes back on the road, but I could feel my heartbeat quicken.

Was it possible that Manny did know something? And did that mean . . .

Oh my God.

No, no, no, no, no, no, no.

Don't say it, Charlie. Don't even think it.

But I couldn't help it. Was it possible that I liked J.D.?!!

This was *so* not in the plan.

Thirty-Four

I rushed into school Friday morning and headed straight for the main office. There was a little desk outside of it that had sign-up sheets, pamphlets, and most important—the paper. I picked up a copy.

The cover page looked nice; it was about volunteering over the holidays and had pictures of students at a nursing home and another of the soccer team helping out at a soup kitchen over Thanksgiving.

I thumbed through the next few pages. So far so good. I kept flipping. I really wanted to see the photo spread. *It had better not be a giant photo of me with a poinsettia plant on my head.*

I opened to the center page and readied myself for the worst. Only it wasn't.

It was incredible. Roughly one hundred photos filled the page, but they weren't just thrown on there. They were carefully placed to form a snowflake. From a distance you wouldn't even be able to tell that it was a photo collage, but up close you could see all of our classmates doing everything from reading in study hall and performing in the school play to hanging out after homecoming and getting the winning touchdown in the football game. The snowflake had six points—and at the very end of each one was a photo of me. The unfortunate aforementioned one of me at the mall, one of Morgan and me cheering at the football game, another of us at Scobell's afterward, one of me decorating J.D.'s Christmas tree, one of me in that ridiculous Christmas spirit costume laughing and singing with a group of children, and one of my snow angel alongside J.D.'s. While that technically wasn't me, it was still my form. And smack in the center of the snow-flake was a picture of me looking out at the town from atop the hill he brought me to. I didn't even know J.D. took a photo of me there.

I couldn't stop staring at the page. "I can't believe he did this."

"What?" someone walking past asked.

"Nothing," I said.

But it wasn't nothing. It was huge. By the end of the day J.D. had taken over all of my thoughts. In class, when I saw him I had a brain freeze. I didn't know what to say. I just smiled and said, "Good job, and don't be late to the party, you promised." Then I barely waited for him to say, "I'll be there" before I pretended to study my book. That wasn't even close to how I wanted it to go down, but I was nervous, and that feeling only tripled itself by the time the *Sentinel* party started. I still wasn't sure what to make of J.D. and his photo spread. Was it his way of telling me he liked me or was he just going with some artistic vision and trying for symmetry?

That's probably it. He said he doesn't want me. I need to stop thinking about him. I don't want him, either. Or do I?

I clutched the bag I was holding. It had both J.D.'s and Teo's gifts inside. Teo . . . Why wasn't I focusing more on Teo? The past several weeks had all been leading up to today. I needed to get my head in the game.

Noelle's birthday party was just days away, and I was going to have a date. Not just a date, the perfect date. *Teo.* He was the one that would make Zakiyah's head spin. But what did I care what she thought of me—or my date?

I walked into the computer room right on time, and Teo was already there. He saw me and smiled, that smile that exuded confidence and charm. It wasn't cocky or smug or accompanied by a giant, distracting dimple like his cousin's. It was so much better. Of course it was.

I took a deep breath and made my way over to him. He met me halfway, in front of Morgan's massive dessert display. I had brought in a bunch of drinks, but she brought in homemade fudge, lollipops, and no less than a dozen different types of cookies. She had spent her last-period study hall setting it all up. And people thought I was the overachiever.

"Hey," Teo said.

"Hey," I repeated back to him.

His eyes did a quick glance down my body, and I found myself shifting away from him. I had worn the dark-green dress because

234

it brought out my eyes, and I liked the sleek A-line fit. I wanted him to notice, so why all of a sudden did it feel wrong?

J.D., that's why.

But someone who liked me wouldn't be late to my party, not when he knew how much that bothered me. I looked at the door. No sign of him.

I took one of Morgan's candy cane cookies and studied the red-and-white twists. "She's really good at what she does," I said.

He picked up a green Rice Krispies treat wreath. "That's probably part of why you get along so well. You're both at the top of your game."

"You're one to talk."

"That's why we get along so well, too."

I raised an eyebrow at him. I had barely seen him since he gave me the gift on Monday. We'd passed each other in the hall maybe three times and didn't even speak. "Do we?" I asked. "We never talk."

"That's something we need to change." He patted the present he was holding. "I thought about you a lot this week, and I found you something I think you're going to love."

"Yeah?"

"Yep, you'll see when you open it. I'd let you sneak a peek now, but I know you like to play by the rules."

That was true, and in the e-mail I sent out, I specifically said that the final present exchange would take place at the end of the party—one hour in, when we would all open our presents together.

I was so confused. When Teo wanted to, he could ooze charm and make me feel like we could really be something incredible together. And here he was, trying to make an effort, making my power-couple dream seem like it could be a reality, and all I could do was look over his shoulder, hoping his cousin would walk in. What was going on with me?

"Teo," Bobby said, walking over. "Thanks for doing the article. It really beefed up the sports section."

As they talked about the championship game, I slipped away and sank into a chair in the back corner. There were enough monitors in front of me to keep me virtually hidden. Which was what I needed. I could not face Zakiyah right now. I just needed to think.

"Here you are," Morgan said, taking a seat next to me a little while later. "I've been searching all over for you. What's wrong?"

"I don't know."

I looked between the screens at the party for what had to be the eightieth time. My eyes went from Teo to the door. Still no J.D.

"Looking for someone?" she asked.

"No."

She knew I was, but she also knew not to push. I did not want to cry. Not here. Not in front of everyone. "He's always late," was all she said about it. She held out a little plate, and I took one of the three sugar cookies on it. "But I saw you talking to Teo. That's good, right?"

"Yeah, I guess so."

"What is it?"

"It's just . . ." I shook my head. "I just don't know if he gets me."

"I thought you two were 'perfect,'" she said, quoting my words from before back to me.

"Maybe I was wrong." I picked at the cookie. "I don't know. He got me these amazing presents that show he listened to what I had to say. Don't get me wrong, that's a huge plus, but other than being coeditor of the paper, a straight-A student, someone who hangs out with his cousin, likes cats, marshmallows, and red flowers, I'm not sure he has any idea who I am."

I looked over at Teo. He was talking to a group of five people, and they were all laughing and hanging on to his every word. Everyone was having a great time, while I hid and kept a secret watch on the door. I was being crazy.

"Would there be somebody else perchance who does?" Morgan asked. Then she quickly added, "Not that I'm naming any names."

I looked at the clock on the wall. "Apparently not." We were just shy of an hour into the party, and J.D. still hadn't made an appearance. He had broken his promise. "We should go do the gift exchange. It's almost time."

I waited another two minutes and then called everyone to attention and launched into my prepared remarks. "Thank you all for coming out today and helping us celebrate not only the holidays, but the holiday edition of the paper. You put a lot of hard work into it, and I know I may have been difficult at times . . ." I paused as Zakiyah and a few others snickered. When I rehearsed the speech, I had planned to look at J.D. when I said that part and smile—now it felt flat. "But," I continued, "it all paid off. It looks amazing, and you all did an incredible job. Thank you. And now what you've all been waiting for. It's time for the big Secret Santa reveal—go ahead and give your last gift. We have the room for another fifteen minutes, and then we have to get out of here so the staff can start their winter break, too. So enjoy the rest of the party, happy holidays, and thank you again."

Teo held his present up and walked over to me.

"Guess it's not much of a reveal," I said.

"How's this then—I actually pulled Gus's name but traded it for yours."

"Really?"

He wanted to get my name?

"Wait," I said, thinking back to the drawing. "You were sitting next to Zakiyah, weren't you? She was asking about a trade."

"Guilty," he confessed.

"Then it wasn't like you wanted to get me; you were only helping her out."

"Who said the two are mutually exclusive? I can help someone *and* get what I want, can't I?" he asked.

"I suppose."

"At least I put in a little effort; you only got my name by luck," he said. "That still puts me ahead of the curve."

If he only knew.

"So are we doing this?" he asked, raising his eyebrows up and down and pointing to the bag I was holding.

He was sweet. Why was I being so weird? This was what I wanted. "Yes," I said and handed him a little gift bag, ignoring the one for J.D.

The baseball was covered by about three pounds of tissue paper. Teo tore into it and pulled out his present. "Is this really . . . ? No. You didn't! Did you?! You got me a signed Manny Franco ball?"

I had seen him get excited over the other gifts, but those reactions were nothing in comparison to this. Those gifts were like stale fruitcake. This was like Santa struck gold. Teo actually picked me up and spun me around. Everyone turned to look, although he didn't seem to care. But Zakiyah definitely took notice. I just smiled at her and turned away, but I knew she was fuming. I had won. Yet I didn't feel like a winner.

Okay, I needed to get out of this funk. It wasn't like I even wanted J.D., I reminded myself. I was just disappointed he broke his promise about being there, that was all. We were supposed to be friends.

"Charlie, this is incredible," Teo said. "Thank you. Come here." We walked over to a seat by the side of the room, and he handed me the wrapped gift he was holding. "Open yours. It was made especially for you."

The way he was looking at me, that's what I wanted, that's what I deserved. I ripped open the paper. It was a weekly planner. The cover had two kittens playing in the snow.

"Look inside," he said.

There were little drawings and handwritten inscriptions written there. One page in December said, *Remember to schedule time for yourself—a long walk or car ride*, and it had a little car next to it. Another blocked off two hours for leisure reading and had a drawing of a book and hearts. And on January first,

New Year's Day was crossed off, and it said, *Charlie's Day*, and it had a birthday cake, balloons, and streamers around it. I hadn't even remembered telling him about my birthday. He must have found it on my GroupIt page. The whole calendar was filled with things like that. October had notes like *stop stressing about college applications, you're brilliant, you've got this.*

I looked up at Teo in awe. "You did this?"

He shrugged. "I wanted something to impress you."

"Teo, thank you so much." I reached over and gave him a hug, and he squeezed me back tightly. I had been so wrong. He did know me. He knew exactly what I needed.

"Hey," Katie shouted. "Where's my gift?"

"J.D. must have your name," Bobby said, still holding a wrapped present. "He's not here."

So typical. How had I ever thought that I liked J.D. better than his cousin?

I turned my attention back to Teo. "Any chance you want to go with me to Noelle's party?" And I wasn't inviting him because of Zakiyah, or J.D., or just to have a date. I was asking because he was the right guy for me. A guy who was there for me, a guy who did what he said he was going to do, a guy who spent what had to be hours upon hours making me a gift he knew I'd love. That was who I wanted to be with.

"Yes," he said, putting his hand on mine. "I was hoping you'd ask."

It was true what they said, great minds really did think alike.

Thirty-Five

On Christmas Eve, Mom and I went to midnight mass. I should have been happy. The ceremony was beautiful, I was spending time with my mother, after next week her work schedule was going to be a lot lighter, and the date I had been dreaming about for weeks was actually going to happen. Everything was going the way I wanted. So why wasn't I more excited?

"Merry Christmas, sweetie," my mother said as we walked to the car.

"Merry Christmas."

"Are you okay?" she asked.

"Yeah, I'm fine." It wasn't technically a lie. There wasn't anything actually wrong with me. I just felt a little empty, but I didn't want to talk about it, so when we got to the car, I turned the radio on to some Christmas music and pretended everything was great.

"You know," my mom said as we walked into the house, "since

it *is* technically Christmas morning, we could open presents now. I say we change into comfy pajamas and meet back at the tree in five!"

She looked so excited that I couldn't help but smile back at her and agree.

"Look what I have," she said, her face all mischievous, when I reentered the living room. She held up a tray of spicy cinnamon rolls. "It's never too early for cream cheese frosting, right?"

"Right," I said and took a big bite of one. But it was just for Mom's benefit. I wasn't really in the mood to eat.

"Okay," she said, handing me a box. "Open this one first, since you already know what it is." Inside was a brochure for the summer program I went to every year. "You can pick a different one if you prefer."

"This one is awesome, thank you," I said.

"That's not all."

We opened up a bunch of little gifts. Blouses, earrings, Christmas socks—the ones she got me had reindeer on them and the nose was a little red cotton ball that protruded from it. They reminded me of J.D.'s ugly Christmas sweater. *I bet he'd love these.* I kicked myself. He wasn't supposed to creep into my thoughts. I wasn't in his. All I got from him was a one-sentence text on Friday that said: *I'm really sorry I missed the party.* No explanation. No "please forgive me" pleas. No phone call. I didn't respond, and he didn't reach out again.

"Now the grand finale," Mom announced with fanfare in her voice. We always saved the best presents for last.

"Me first," I said, handing her an envelope.

"Charlie, this is perfect." It was a gift certificate for a mother-daughter day at the spa. I wanted something we could do together.

"We are going to use this ASAP. Now open yours," she said. It was a small jewelry box, but when I opened it, it wasn't jewelry; two tickets unfurled. Mom had had a similar idea. "I thought we could go away during your spring recess. Just you and me. Florida. The beach, Disney World, Epcot, whatever you want. I already put in for the time off."

I had been dying to go away forever. I hugged her. "Thank you, this is really amazing." I traced my fingers over the tickets. Too bad we couldn't take off right now.

"Charlotte Donovan," she said, studying me. "What's going on with you?"

"Nothing. I'm excited. I love the gifts. I love that we're going on a trip. Really."

Mom shook her head. "No. Something's up. The Charlie I know would be screaming about these tickets by now."

She was right. Don't get me wrong, I truly was thrilled with the gift, I just wasn't in the mood to jump up and down. Everything seemed sort of muted.

"Talk to me," she said.

And I did. I told her everything. About Teo, and how J.D. had gone from the most annoying guy on the planet to a guy I actually liked spending time with, and how he let me down. And how I should have been over the moon between my upcoming date and spending Christmas Eve with her and getting all these presents, but I was kind of sad.

She put her arm around me. "I'm sorry, sweetie. Maybe J.D. had a good reason for missing the party."

"Doubt it," I said. If he did, he would have told me already. Or at least made more of an effort to apologize. He knew I really wanted him there.

"Well, even if he didn't, don't let him ruin your Christmas. You said it yourself, you have all these wonderful things to look forward to—focus on that. Now come on." She picked up the tray of cinnamon rolls and headed toward her room. (Christmas was the one time a year she allowed eating in the bedroom.) "We have some Christmas movie watching to do."

She was right, I had to appreciate what I had. We crawled into her bed and turned on *A Christmas Story*. It played on TV for twenty-four hours straight. Mom had already fallen asleep by the time Ralphie came out in the pink bunny suit. I shut the television off when I saw it. I didn't need a reminder of the caroling night. Instead, I went to my room and got out the planner Teo had made for me.

This is what I need to concentrate on.

The detail and time that went into it was unbelievable. Teo really cared. J.D. couldn't even bother to show up. I held the planner close to my chest and took a deep breath.

I was definitely going to Noelle's party with the right Ortiz cousin; the proof was in my hands.

Thirty-Six

"Merry Christmas!" Morgan said when I stopped by her house late Christmas afternoon. Since my mom had to work, I decided to join Morgan's family for a movie. "How was the holiday?" she asked.

"It was okay. Not my best ever, but there were a lot of good things," I said and filled her in on the highlights, like my upcoming trip.

"And did you hear from . . . ?" she asked, her voice dipping out at the end.

I pulled at my ponytail. "Teo texted. Wished me a Merry Christmas, and we made plans to meet tomorrow for Noelle's party."

"That's great. But I, um, actually meant J.D.," she said, her voice soft.

I shook my head, and Morgan bit her lip.

"It's fine," I told her, but she scrunched her eyes closed and wrung her hands together. I felt my stomach sink. Something was up. "*Morgan*, what did you do?"

She opened one eye. "Nothing. Well, not intentionally. Okay, don't be mad, but I ran into him outside last night, and I might have yelled at him for not showing up at the party and stuff like that."

I yanked my hair so hard it hurt. "What do you mean *stuff like that?*"

"Don't worry, I didn't tell him you like him."

This was not happening. "I *don't* like him."

"You're right, I'm sorry. I just told him how disappointed we *both* were that he didn't show up. That he promised you, and it was crappy for him to bail. That's all."

I let out a sigh. "Okay." I guess that wasn't so bad. "And what did he say?"

"He felt really horrible. I believed him. Really. He said he wanted to apologize and make it up to you, and—"

The doorbell cut her off.

"And I may have told him you'd be over at my house today," she said superfast. "Don't kill me, and give him a chance, he really looked sorry." She didn't wait for my response as she went to answer the door.

I knew it was Christmas and goodwill and peace and all— but I was going to murder her.

Morgan opened the door, and there was J.D. She gave him a hug and wished him a Merry Christmas. He looked right at me, and I just stood there, not knowing what to do.

"Come in," Morgan told him. "Can I get you some leftover *Sentinel* party cookies? They're all yours, if you want them."

"Actually, I just have a minute. I have to get back to my family, but I saw Charlie's car in the driveway and wanted to stop by for a second."

"Sure. You know, I, um, think I left the stove on. I better go check it."

Real subtle, Morgan.

She left, and it was just the two of us. "Merry Christmas," he said.

"Same," I answered. What did he want from me?

He shuffled back and forth on his feet, and I stayed planted. Waiting.

Finally, he spoke again. "I just wanted to apologize for missing the *Sentinel* party the other day. I didn't mean to."

"Can't say I was surprised," I said, my eyes studying the floor. "It's not like you cared about it anyway."

"That's not true."

"Whatever, it's fine. Your spread in the paper looked great, that's what matters."

"I didn't miss the party on purpose," he blurted out. "I was talking to my grandfather."

"And it had to be during the party?"

"Actually," he paused and his eyes got a faraway look. "It did. I told you he moved to be near my aunt because he couldn't take the winters here. That's true, but he's also been having a hard time with his memory, and my aunt is in a better position to take care of him." His eyes welled up. "This sounds strange, but he's like my best friend in the world. He taught me to love art, to take a good picture, to paint, to solder, to cut glass, to not miss what's right in front of you." He smiled as he spoke. "I would see him almost every other day when he lived around here. When he moved we switched to FaceTime." J.D. got quiet again. "You saw him the night of the ugly sweater party. He was okay that night, but he does better during the day; it's like he's more there, more himself. So we have a routine. I call him after school most days. Sometimes the conversation is a couple of minutes. Sometimes it goes a lot longer, and it makes me run behind for other things."

That was why he was always late for the *Sentinel* meetings? I didn't know what to say.

J.D. kept talking. "On Friday, he was having a really good day. It was like old times, and he was in this really talkative mood. I wanted to be at the party, but I couldn't say good-bye to him. It was so close to Christmas, and he was like his old self."

Now I felt like I was tearing up. "Why didn't you tell me?"

He shrugged. "It's not something that's easy for me to talk about."

"But all those times I gave you a hard time for being late, you could have just said you had something beforehand."

"I was afraid you would have pushed for an explanation." He bowed his head slightly. "It wasn't something I was ready to give."

He was right. I would have pushed.

"Anyway," he said, "I really did want to be there. I was planning on giving this to you, too." He handed me a small bag. "I saw the way you were looking at the ornaments my family made, and I thought maybe you and your mom could start a tradition of your own."

"Thanks," I said. My stomach felt like it was forming a pretzel. J.D. had been going through a lot, and I had just jumped to conclusions about him. And yet, here he was still being thoughtful. The doorbell rang again.

"It's probably for me," he said as Morgan appeared from the kitchen. "My mom warned me if I wasn't back in five minutes, she was sending out the troops to track me down."

Morgan laughed and headed toward the door.

J.D. turned his focus back to me. "So . . . I hear Operation Secret Santa worked."

"Yeah, we did it," I said, but even though J.D. helped make it a reality, it felt strange talking about it with him. "It was a success. Teo and I are going to the party together."

"I know. He told me."

The doorbell rang again.

I looked over at Morgan. She had totally been spying. She quickly turned her attention from me and J.D. to the door.

She opened it—and it was none other than Teo himself.

Speak of the devil.

Morgan let him in, and they both walked over to me and J.D.

"Hey there," Teo said, putting his arm around my shoulder. "Merry Christmas."

"Merry Christmas."

It felt a little awkward. Morgan must have sensed it, too. "You guys want to all go sit in the living room?" she asked. "It's more comfortable."

Teo didn't seem to notice anything weird. "I would, but my aunt won't serve dessert until we're back, and Dylan is going crazy. I was sent to get J.D. before my brother has a Christmas meltdown."

"Poor kid," Morgan said. "I know the power of dessert."

With that, we all said our good-byes, and I watched the Ortiz cousins walk away.

"Wow," Morgan said, still staring at the door. "Just wow."

"What?" I asked.

"*What?*" she mimicked me, as she walked into the living room and dropped onto the couch. "Did you not hear the same conversation that I did? I'm talking about J.D." I knew she had been eavesdropping. Not that it mattered; I would have told her everything anyway. "He really likes you."

I sank down next to her. "Clearly you were spying on someone else, because he said nothing of the sort."

"Charlie, he even bought you a present!"

"So, you did, too—it doesn't mean anything." I was still clutching onto the bag he had given me.

"It does. Open it," she said. "I want to see."

"Fine." I reached inside, carefully pulled out the contents, and let out a slight gasp. It was an ornament—a figurine of my mom holding me when I was a baby in front of our Christmas tree.

"I posted this picture on GroupIt last year," I said, staring in awe at the detailing. It was one of the few pictures I had ever put up. It was always one of my favorites, and now J.D. had brought it to life.

250

"That's incredible," Morgan said.

"It really is." He must have 3-D printed it at his internship. "I can't believe he did this for me." The Ortiz boys definitely knew how to give a gift.

"Okay, this proves I'm right," Morgan said, nodding in approval. "He is head over heels for you."

"No. It means he looks at me as a good friend. He helped set me up with his *cousin*. Or did you forget that part?"

"And did *you* forget that he made you the focal point of his whole photo spread? I can't believe I didn't realize this ages ago," she said. "You guys are supposed to be together. The initial fighting was just because you were trying to deny your chemistry. It's so obvious to me now."

She needed to stop. My life wasn't some fairy tale or storybook romance. "Morgan, you watch too much TV. He doesn't like me; he *laughed* at the idea of us being together. And if you want to go the whole Hallmark movie route, I think Teo is much more the classic leading man. The guy has his choice of colleges and has just about everything going for him. He's definitely the smarter pick."

"Charlie!" She shook her arms in the air. "Picking who you like isn't the same as picking which school or summer program you should attend. You need to go with your feelings, not some checklist. J.D. could be the perfect boyfriend if you gave him a chance."

"He doesn't want a chance, Morgan. J.D is not shy; if he wanted me, he would have said it. Instead, he helped me win over his cousin—which is what I want, it's what I've wanted from the start. Teo isn't just practical. He's amazing. He understands me. He's the type of guy I should have in my life."

"See!" she cried.

"See what?"

"You said he's the type of guy you *should* have in your life—not the type of guy you *want* in your life."

"Enough," I cried out. "I *want* Teo. Teo. Teo. Teo. There, happy?"

"Okay." She held up her hands in surrender. "I'm sorry. It's just, you know I've always thought J.D. was kind of awesome, and I just got excited about the idea of the two of you together. But I'll stop. I get it, you like Teo. Not J.D."

"Thank you," I said.

I wasn't sure she really believed it.

But I did.

I had to.

Thirty-Seven

Noelle's extravaganza started at seven, and I, naturally, wanted to be there right on the dot. I picked up Teo at his house. "Wow," he said when he got in the car. "You look really pretty."

"Thanks, you look really good, too."

This was it. I was on the way to Noelle's with Teo. I had done it. I had gotten what I wanted. Operation Secret Santa was a success. I wanted to be more excited. *This is Morgan's fault.* She put in my head that J.D. had feelings for me, but I knew that wasn't true, and besides, it didn't matter. I had Teo, and he was great. "How was your Christmas?" I asked him.

"Great, yours?"

"Really nice," I said.

The conversation the rest of the drive was just as stilted. This was supposed to be my dream date with my dream guy, yet a simple conversation was torturous.

I was relieved when we made it inside the party and Noelle ran over. She was holding on to her boyfriend's hand, and he had to jog to keep up. "You're here," she said. "I knew I could count on you to be here on time. And," she said, raising her eyebrows up and down at Teo, "to follow my directions." She was talking about bringing a date, but really, this whole party, this whole couple's theme seemed kind of stuffy. I kind of wished the party was more like a few years ago—where everyone hung out in a big group and it didn't matter who was with whom. Everyone just had a good time.

"Noelle, Lee, you know Teo, right?" I asked.

"Not formally," she said, and stuck out her hand so he could shake it. "I'm glad you could come to the Lovers' Ball."

Did she really call it that out loud? To Teo? I tried not to cringe.

We made small talk for a bit, and when a few more people walked in, Noelle and Lee went off to greet them.

"Should we get a drink?" I asked.

"Sure," he said. "I promise not to spike it."

His words made me think of J.D.—the way he helped me after I got drunk. He had been so nice. *Stop it, Charlie. You're here with Teo. Enjoy it.* We walked over to the bar. I had to give Noelle credit. The place was even more decked out than last year. There was a giant ice sculpture that spelled out Noelle's name, Christmas lights galore, flower arrangements the size of small trees, two bars that served nonalcoholic drinks (and after my eggnog mishap, I was more than fine with that), and six food stations—sushi, mashed potato bar, a meat carving station, personally prepared pasta dishes, sliders, and a raw bar. There was also mistletoe over every doorway, although I pretended not to notice that.

I felt like my dress was closing in around me. I tugged at the collar. Why was I so uncomfortable?

"You okay?" Teo asked.

I nodded and took my soda from the bartender.

Heather spotted us and waved. "Teo, Charlie," she said, coming over. "I made the list after all. Although I think you were right about Kevin Wayward. I don't think he's showing, but I'm keeping my fingers crossed he pops up and performs at some point anyway. Still, this party is like nothing I've ever seen. I mean, there are a million little tables for two, and each one has *two dozen* roses. Not that I want to sit at my table for two."

"Why not?" Teo asked.

"You know how bad I wanted to come to this, right?" she said. We both nodded.

"Okay, so don't judge me. But the girl who was supposed to come with one of Noelle's cousins decided she'd rather stay home, so I got to take her place."

"What's so bad about that?" I asked.

Her face scrunched up in embarrassment. "He's fourteen."

Teo spit out part of his drink and started laughing. "You're on a date with a freshman!"

She got one of the twins.

"It is not a date. We didn't even come together. I'm just assigned to a table with him, and I promised one dance."

I could see why the other girl backed out. Didn't sound like a stellar evening. I had met the twins, and unless they had completely changed in one year's time, they were not the most mature guys in their class.

"Hey!" She swatted Teo. "Stop laughing. It was the only way I could come. The only non-juniors invited were the dates of those who were and Noelle's family. But did you see that shrimp over there? That alone makes this night worth it." Then she kind of maneuvered herself behind me. "There he is. Hide me."

Noelle's cousin was headed our way.

"You know, I think I'm going to run to the restroom," she said.

Pretty soon Teo and I were alone again.

"I can't believe she agreed to come with him," he said.

"I know."

"Any guy would have taken her if she'd asked; she didn't have to go with Noelle's cousin," he added.

I waited for the surge of jealousy to hit me, but oddly, it didn't come.

For the next few moments we just stood there sipping our drinks. It was strange. For weeks, all I'd wanted was for Heather to leave me alone with Teo, and now that she had, I kind of wished she was still with us.

I looked around the room. There was no sign of Morgan and Ira. Or J.D. I guessed he'd decided not to come. But I did see Zakiyah staring at me. Here it was, my big moment, my chance to rub it in her face that I scored the perfect date, yet it just seemed petty and kind of pathetic now. I turned away.

Another slow song started playing. "Want to dance?" Teo asked.

"Yeah, okay."

We moved out onto the dance floor, and he put his arms around my waist, but this time I didn't feel any of that electric jolt I used to get around him. And let's face it, I knew why. It was J.D. My mind kept going back to him.

For the millionth time, snap out of it, Charlie! This is what you wanted. Teo is the smart decision, and *he's the one who wanted to be here.* He had been incredibly sweet to me. I needed to think about that. This was *Teo.* Teo who gave me all those thoughtful gifts. Teo who knew about my little idiosyncrasies, and instead of writing me off, wrote cute little notes about them in an organizer calendar.

"You know," I said as we swayed back and forth to the music, "all of those things you wrote in the calendar, I love them. I've already been through it at least a dozen times. And those drawings. They're incredible."

He didn't respond, so I kept on going. "You're really talented. What kinds of other stuff do you draw?"

He cocked his head slightly to the side. "I actually don't," he said.

"Huh?" I waited for him to go on.

"I can't draw," he admitted.

I stopped moving. "What are you talking about? You said you made the planner especially for me."

He got a sheepish grin. "Actually, I said it *was* made special. You sort of assumed I did it myself, and I may have let you."

Ice-cold shivers ran down my body. "Well, who *actually* made it?"

"J.D. may have helped me with the gifts."

I dropped my hands from his shoulders.

My mind was racing. "Wait a minute, *gifts*? Plural. When you say he helped you . . . how much of it was him?" I took a step back.

Teo looked like he was considering how much to confess. "Now don't forget, he helped you pick out presents, too." Then he let out a sigh. "He pretty much did it all."

"So everything . . . the gifts, the notes, and the drawings in the planner . . . they were all J.D.?" I asked. I was kind of scared and excited for the answer.

"I gave the seal of approval on his ideas, but yeah, it was him. He's better at that type of stuff, and he wanted to make some little drawings, so I figured why not."

It wasn't just drawings, it was what was behind them.

Oh my God.

The Gerbera daisy? The marshmallow kittens? The five golden rings? The planner? All the moments that really showed how much Teo paid attention and understood me, and they were all from J.D.?!!?

I started pacing around the dance floor. "Ohmygodohmygod ohmygod."

It was J.D. It was always J.D.

"Charlie?" Teo said.

But I couldn't focus. I just started babbling. "Was Morgan right? Does J.D. . . . ? No. Maybe? He did all of that for me. Ohmy godohmygod."

"You really like him," Teo said quietly. I wasn't sure if he was asking or telling.

I stopped pacing. "I'm sorry. I thought he didn't care. And I—"

"You should go talk to him," Teo said.

That rush of excitement I was missing earlier had arrived. "Yeah?"

He smiled at me. "Yeah."

I was about to leave when I realized something. "Wait. How are you going to get home? I drove you here."

"I'll figure it out," he said. "Go."

"Really?"

"Get out of here. You should be with him," he said.

I gave him a giant hug. "Thank you."

On my way to the coat check, Heather stopped me. "Are you okay?" she asked. I must have looked more than a little frenzied. Although she didn't seem so great herself. She was sitting at a little table alone and looking miserable.

"Yeah, I just have to go," I told her.

"What about Teo? Where is he?"

"He's right over there," I said, pointing to where I left him, about ten feet away. He saw us, and I got an idea. Maybe everyone could get their happily ever after tonight.

I waved Teo over. "Heather, can you do me a favor and give this guy a ride home?" I asked when he got there.

"What?! Yeah, of course." Her face instantly lit up.

"Great," I told her. "And just so you know, Noelle sucks at matchmaking, but I don't. So say hi to your new date."

I didn't stick around to watch what happened next, I had my own story to finish.

Thirty-Eight

My heart was racing as I ran to the coatroom. Morgan and Ira were just walking out.

"I'm sorry. I'm using my late pass," Morgan said. "We were—"

"It's fine, it's fine," I told her as I grabbed my jacket. "I have to leave anyway."

"What? Where are you going?" she asked.

"To J.D.'s. You were right, Morgan. He's the one. I'll explain everything later. I promise."

"I expect a call ASAP," she yelled after me. "I want to hear everything! And good luck!"

I jumped in my car. I knew exactly what I needed to do.

I parked in front of J.D.'s house and grabbed the gift bag with his present. It had been sitting in my car since Friday. I was shaking as I walked up his walkway. What if I was too late? What if going to the party with Teo ruined everything? What if he didn't want anything to do with me anymore? I paused in front of the door and took a deep breath. I was doing it regardless. If J.D. showed me anything, it was that sometimes you just had to go with your gut.

I rang the bell, and J.D.'s sister opened the door.

"Is J.D. home?" I asked.

She told me he was out on the back porch, and I went to go see him.

His back was to me, and he was holding his camera toward the sky. It was a perfect winter night. A beautiful dark sky full of stars. I made a wish on one.

"J.D.?" I said.

"Charlie?" He turned around. "What are you doing here? Why aren't you at Noelle's party?"

I couldn't read his expression. Was he happy to see me or not? Confessing my feelings was going to be a lot harder than I thought. I held up the bag I was holding. "Well, you gave me so many amazing presents, I thought I could at least give you one."

"So many?"

I took a step closer to him. "I know it was you behind everything. Why didn't you tell me? Why would you do that for him?"

"I didn't do it for him, I did it for *you*. I knew Teo had your name in the Secret Santa, and after you told me you got a broken candy cane, I knew the gifts weren't going to get any better and how crushed you would be when you found out they were from Teo. So I offered to help him out."

"But you couldn't stand me back then, and you still did that?"

He put his camera down on a little table near us. "You drove

261

me crazy at the *Sentinel*, but the more time I spent with . . . I don't know. You're so smart and determined and you say what's on your mind and you're passionate about everything you do. It's sexy."

Did he just call me sexy!? And did this mean what I thought it meant?

I couldn't take it anymore. "If I'm so great," I blurted out, "then why did you help set me up with your cousin?"

"Because I promised you I would." He smiled that smile of his, his giant dimple showing. "But I did try to sabotage my efforts. Crazy costumes and ugly sweaters. I was hoping it would scare Teo off, but you charmed him."

"I think *your gifts* charmed him," I said, clutching the bag I brought. "They charmed me. You should have told me the truth."

"I didn't think you wanted it. You built Teo up to be the perfect person for you."

"You might want to mark this occasion," I told him, "because here's something you don't hear every day from me. I was wrong. Very wrong. He's not the one I want."

He was watching me, but I still couldn't tell what he was thinking.

"I got you something," I said and handed him the bag. I watched him take out his present. It was a twist on what I did for Morgan. I had taken the photos J.D. shot and posted on his GroupIt page and created his own photography book. He looked back up at me. "Charlie." His voice was soft. "You made this?"

I nodded. "I brought it to the *Sentinel* party, but then . . ."

"Then I didn't show."

"I hated that you weren't there. I was really upset. More than I knew what to do with," I confessed.

"I wanted to be there."

I rested my hand on the table. "I know, and you had a good reason. I just wish you had told me about it sooner."

"I was going to. I got off the phone right after the party and headed straight there, but I ran into Teo on the way. He told me you'd asked him to Noelle's. I realized I needed to back off."

"No, you didn't. I was just being stupid." It was time to be bold. "I should never have gone to the party with Teo. It was you I wanted, but I was afraid to admit it. To you. To me. To Morgan. To Teo. I knew it at Manny's and then when I saw your photo spread . . ." I looked right at him, hoping he could see how much I cared. "I can't believe you did that. It was gorgeous."

He put his hand on the table, his fingertips touching mine. "Well, look who I had for a muse."

My whole body felt warm.

Our eyes were still locked, and my breathing was getting heavy. It was now or never. I put my hand on top of his. "Does this mean you forgive me?"

J.D. laced his fingers with mine. "I think it does," he said.

The next instant, he wrapped his arm around me, and I was melting into his kiss. Forget an electric jolt. This was shooting stars, Christmas morning, first-place trophies, early Harvard acceptances, and fireworks all rolled into one. I never wanted the feeling to stop.

My wish had come true.

J.D. was everything I didn't know I wanted—or needed—but did. I reached my arms around him and pulled him even closer. As his lips pressed deeply into mine, I knew I had finally gotten the perfect Christmas gift.

Acknowledgments

This book was a lot of fun to write, and I am so thankful to everyone who helped make it a possibility.

To everyone at Swoon Reads and Macmillan—thank you, thank you, thank you! Holly West and Lauren Scobell, I am very grateful for your support, feedback, and enthusiasm. You made this an amazing experience. To Jonathan Yaged, Jean Feiwel, Emily Settle, Kristin Dulaney, and everyone in subrights; Caitlin Sweeney, Caitlin Crocker, and everyone in digital; Kathryn Little, Ashley Woodfolk, Teresa Ferraiolo, and everyone in marketing; Allison Verost, Kelsey Marrujo, and the whole publicity team; Mariel Dawson and the advertising team; Jenn Gonzalez, Claire Taylor, and everyone in sales; production editor Ilana Worrell and copyeditor Jill Amack; and to everyone else involved with this book, you've all been incredible. Thank you again for everything.

Liz Dresner, who designed the cover (with a special shout-out to Holly and her knitting skills)—it's awesome, thank you!

To the Swoon community, I learn from you every day and appreciate all of your support and feedback.

Laura Dail, I feel so lucky to have you in my corner. Thank you for always having my back.

The librarians, booksellers, bloggers, reviewers, and readers, thank you for letting Charlie and co. into your lives.

To my colleagues and friends at Fox 5, your support does not go unnoticed. Thank you for being there for me. To the rest of my friends and family—the same applies to you. I couldn't do this without you. Thank you.

Mom, Jordan, Andrea, Liam, and Alice—I grow more in awe of you all every day. When it comes to family, I definitely hit the jackpot. I love you. And to my father, whom I greatly miss, I know my love for books and the written word is largely due to you. I love you for that and so much more.

And to the cast of the theater tour I was on many years ago— thank you for humoring me when I really wanted to have a holiday party and do a Secret Santa. It not only helped inspire this book but also gave me a lot of great memories.

FEELING BOOKISH?

Turn the page for some

Swoonworthy EXTRAS

A New Year
(Deleted Scene)

I looked at my phone. Again. What was taking J.D. so long? "He's going to miss the countdown."

"He'll be back," Morgan said.

"There's probably just a line," Ira added.

I knew they were right. But still . . . J.D.'s timing sucked. I didn't want to bring in the new year *and* my birthday without him. It was bad enough I was spending the evening at Heather's— but to have to stand there by myself while Ira and Morgan and just about everyone else in the room kissed someone at midnight made it soooo much worse. Technically, I had no right to be grumpy. I was the one who said we should all go to Heather's New Year's Eve party. She had texted me about it no less than two dozen times in the past four days. Since I hooked her and Teo up at Noelle's birthday ball, it was like I was her new best friend. But now that I was here, I kind of wished I wasn't. My birthday officially started in eleven minutes, and I was stuck in a crowded basement with way too much Kevin Wayward music playing and dozens of people I barely knew. I had spent the majority of the party standing in a corner with Morgan, Ira, and J.D.

Only now my date had disappeared. Okay, he went to the bathroom. But at the worst possible time imaginable! This night was a bust. When J.D. had suggested doing something else like having an early birthday celebration, I should have taken him up on it.

Oh well. At least there was tomorrow—which was technically just minutes away. J.D. and I had plans to hang out then. Still, it would have been nice to have celebrated tonight.

"I'm sure he'll be back any second," Morgan said, and squeezed my arm.

I checked my phone. Ten minutes until midnight. I hoped she was right.

But thirty seconds later, a minute, a minute twenty—he still hadn't returned.

"Relax," Morgan said. "There's still plenty of time."

Only there wasn't.

Finally, with seven minutes 'til the countdown, I got a text. *Meet me in the study.*

I showed it to Morgan. Was J.D. crazy? I wasn't wandering around Heather's house and sneaking into rooms. Especially when Heather clearly told everyone the party remains down in the basement. No exceptions.

"What are you waiting for?" Morgan asked.

"We're not supposed to—"

"Go!" she commanded and pointed to the steps.

"Fine." I was going to kill J.D. if he got me in trouble with Heather's parents. I could just picture them calling my mom, and her refusing to ever extend my curfew again.

I marched upstairs. Why did I have to meet him? He should have been coming to me. It was *my* birthday. I didn't even know where the study was. Or why I needed to go there. This night kept getting worse and worse.

I turned down the hall. One of the doors was open. When I walked inside, my annoyance turned to laughter.

J.D. was standing there adorned with a cone birthday hat, party horn, blinking bow tie, and holding a bouquet of colorful helium balloons.

I was at a loss for words. "What?!" was all I could manage to get out.

He blew into the party horn before putting it on the table and saying "Happy birthday!"

"What is all this?" I asked.

"Did you really think I'd ignore your birthday?"

"But we're celebrating tomorrow."

"Who wants to wait that long? I know how important time is to you." He let go of the balloons and pulled out a carton of eggnog from underneath a little table beside him. There were two champagne glasses there and a vase filled with Gerbera daisies. "I thought you might like a surprise."

I took a step closer to him. "You're forgetting, I hate surprises."

He shook his head. "No you don't."

He was right. With J.D., I kind of didn't. He made the unexpected, unexpectedly exciting.

"A toast?" he said and filled the glasses.

"*You* don't like eggnog."

"But you do." It was like Morgan and Ira and the onion rings. J.D. remembered. "And if you want, I bet I can find Teo and see if he has something to add to these."

"Yeah, I'll pass on that one. You know, the snow pretty much melted, and if I can't run out and make angels, it's probably not worth it."

"Probably," J.D. agreed, his face breaking into a smile. I was tempted to reach out and poke his dimple. It was so cute. He handed me one of the glasses.

"J.D., you didn't have to do all this."

"I wanted to. You deserve something special for your birthday."

A month ago, J.D. and I were sparring over newspaper layout, and now here he was being all incredible. How had I not always seen how great he was? I was just thankful I finally came to my senses. "When did you even do all of this? I didn't see any balloons in the car."

"I got here before the party to set up. Heather said I could use the study. She's a pretty big fan of yours right now. And I just thought maybe instead of tonight being about the new year, it should be about you."

He held up his glass. "Now how about that toast?"

"Let's see what you got," I said, laughing.

"Challenge accepted," he said. "To Charlie. Aka baby New Year. Aka the most frustrating, bullheaded taskmaster—"

"You're doing really well here," I interrupted.

"I know how much you love lists," he said, and winked at me. "But you didn't let me finish. And the most beautiful and amazing girl I've ever met."

Only I wasn't the amazing one—he was. I took a sip and put down my glass. J.D. did the same.

"It's almost time," he said, pointing to the clock. It was just seconds away from midnight.

J.D. intertwined his fingers with mine, looked me right in the eyes, and started to count down.

"Ten, nine, eight."

This is seriously the best birthday ever.

"Seven, six, five."

Can I overdose from happiness? Looking at J.D. I feel like I can.

"Four, three, two."

Okay, I can't take it anymore. If he doesn't kiss me soon, I am going to take matters into my own hands.

"One. Happy birthday, Charlie!"

Then it happened.

His lips met mine, and my birthday *and* my year were off to the best possible start.

I had J.D., and the possibilities were endless.

A COFFEE DATE

between author Shani Petroff
and her editor, Holly West

Getting to Know You (A Little More)

Holly West (HW): What book is on your nightstand now?
Shani Petroff (SP): *The Odds of Lightning* by Jocelyn Davies. We were actually in a writing workshop together when she first started working on it, and I'm so excited that it's an actual book now.

HW: What's your favorite word?
SP: That is a tough one. I guess I will go with yes—as in, yes, *My New Crush Gave to Me* is going to be published! (That was a very exciting moment for me.)

HW: If you could travel in time, where would you go and what would you do?
SP: There are the grandiose things I would like to do—fix past travesties, stop horrible acts from happening. And then there are the smaller, more personal things, too—seeing loved ones who have passed away one more time, warning myself of mistakes I will make, etc. Although, there is the concern of how the changes

would alter the present. I have a few book ideas percolating that play with time travel!

HW: Charlie is all about being on time. Are you usually punctual, or are you more like J.D.?
SP: Definitely punctual! I hate being late. Whether it's meetings or deadlines, it's important to me that I'm on time. (And like Charlie, it drives me crazy when someone keeps me waiting—although I'm not quite as obsessive, and give a little more leeway than she does about it!)

HW: *My New Crush Gave to Me* is all about finding the perfect gifts. What's the most perfect gift you've ever received?
SP: Now don't get me wrong, I love a good tangible gift as much as the next person, but my favorite presents are usually more experiential. A special night out or a trip with people that I love always tops my list.

The Swoon Reads Experience (Continues!)

HW: What's your favorite thing about being a Swoon Reads author so far?
SP: It is such a warm community. The support, the feedback, and the camaraderie have all been so incredible. I feel very lucky to be a part of it.

HW: How has the Swoon Reads community impacted your experiences as an author?

SP: It's really enhanced it. It's so nice to hear from people from Swoon Reads and to get their opinions and thoughts—they've become a part of my book family!

HW: Do you have any advice for aspiring authors on the site?
SP: Get involved! Keep writing and submit your work. I also really suggest reading the blog posts (and checking out the archives). There are new posts five days a week, and many of them offer really great advice about writing, editing, getting published, and the whole process.

The Writing Life

HW: Where did you get the inspiration for *My New Crush Gave to Me*?
SP: The idea to do a Christmas book was sparked by Lauren and you! You were both so excited about having one, that it was contagious. The Secret Santa aspect came from a theater tour I was on right after college. We traveled from city to city around the holidays, and like Morgan, I decided it would be fun to do a Secret Santa. The rest of the cast humored me and said okay. It ended up being a blast! And I think I was a really good gift giver, if I do say so myself. ☺

HW: What was the hardest part about writing *My New Crush Gave to Me*?
SP: Coming up with all of the gifts for Teo, Charlie, Charlie's mom, J.D., and Morgan! There were so many of them, and I wanted each

present to be different and special. It took me a lot of time to figure out.

HW: What's your process? Are you an outliner or do you just start at the beginning and make it up as you go?

SP: It depends on the project. I do tend to like outlines, although for this book, I went a different route. I had a really good idea of the plot in my head, and I pulled out a calendar and jotted down the days everything needed to happen—gift giving, parties, caroling, newspaper meetings, etc., and then I just started writing. But generally, I use a more formal chapter-by-chapter outline.

HW: What do you want readers to remember about your books?

SP: My hope for my books like *My New Crush Gave to Me* and *Romeo & What's Her Name* is that readers will think back on them and smile. I personally love romantic comedies; I find them to be a great way to escape for a bit. When I think of my favorites, they make me happy. I remember the laughter and rooting for the lead to get her happily ever after and the content feeling when things end the way they should. And I would love it if my books can do that for people.

FOR NEVER WAS A STORY OF MORE WOE
THAN CRUSHING ON A BOY WHO DOESN'T KNOW

SHANI PETROFF

ROMEO &
WHAT'S HER NAME

Everyone knows understudies never get to perform, but
when Amanda (aka the "real" Juliet) ends up in the hospital,
Emily (aka the COMPLETELY unprepared understudy) has
to star in the most famous scene in Shakespeare's
Romeo and Juliet with the boy of her dreams. Oops?

Jill sent me a text. **Meet me in the bathroom.**

She was already waiting there when I showed up. "Em . . ."

I shook my head. She didn't need to say anything. I could tell by her face. I wasn't going to be Juliet. "You don't need to explain. I was there. I get it. You have to cast Amanda."

"I'm—"

I cut her off. "It's okay. She deserves it. And I know how important this is to you. You have a better shot at best director with her anyway."

Her face looked pained. "I'd still pick you if I could, but she said she'd only accept the part of Juliet, and it's not just my decision." Jill wrapped her arms around herself. "I'm sorry. I know how much you wanted this. And Wes . . ."

"Stop," I said. "It's not your fault. I get it." It sucked, and of course I was upset that I wasn't going to get to work with Wes, but I understood. And I certainly wasn't going to blame Jill for doing what she had to do.

"I just wanted you to hear it from me."

I leaned back against the counter. "Thanks."

"I'm really sorry, Em. If it makes you feel better, even though

I know Amanda is really talented, I'm not looking forward to working with her. Did you see what she did when she passed in her audition sheet? She *patted* me on the head and said, 'You're the lucky little director who gets to work with me.'"

Jill must have been fuming. She hated when people commented on her height. She said there was a lot more to her than her size (which there was) and got majorly annoyed when people referred to her four-foot-ten stature. Amanda knew this. Jill told her off after Amanda made fun of her last year. Clearly, the message didn't sink in. Patting her on the head? That was so patronizing.

"She's horrible," I said. "I can't stand her." I got along with just about everybody at school, yet there was something about Amanda (probably the way she treated everyone) that made me want to scream.

"It gets worse," Jill said. "She stipulated that she'd only take Wes as her Romeo. It's driving me crazy. Who does she think she is? She's not in charge of casting. She is going to be such a pain to work with. Sapna directed her in *The Tempest* last year, and this year she won't even work on the production. Her experience was totally soured. Sapna said she had had enough of the self-entitled, know-it-all Amanda actor-types to fill a lifetime."

I wish I could say I was surprised, but I'd heard Amanda try to control, manipulate, and bully one too many people to think she'd be any other way. "You're a great director, though," I assured Jill. "I know you'll make it work."

"I still wish you were a part of the scene, though. I loved the idea of helping bring you and Wes together. Maybe you can be my assistant or something?"

Being at rehearsals could help, but it wasn't the same as being thought of as Wes's love interest—even if it was just in a play. Then it hit me. "Jill, that's it! You're a genius."

"Huh? Because I want to make you my assistant?"

"No, I'm thinking more of the *or something*. You can make me Amanda's understudy!"

"What? Are you nuts? One-night school performances don't have understudies. Aren't you the one who keeps reminding me this isn't Broadway?"

"Well, maybe that should change."

"Em, no one's going to want to learn all those lines to never get to say them."

"Then don't make *everyone* do it. Just make me," I said.

"So the only person in the whole production who will have an understudy is Amanda?" Jill asked. "She's going to love that one."

"Who cares? She thinks she has all the control. Let's turn it around. Blame it on me. Tell her, tell the directors, tell everyone I really need the extra credit, and there's no other place for me. That they should see me trying to build a set or hang lights. That this will cause the least damage to the production as a whole. They'll understand. They've all seen how klutzy I am. They'll think you're even taking one for the team. Besides, they know we're friends. They won't care. You can even tell Mrs. Heller that my role is understudy/director's assistant. And I will assist you—in whatever you need. I promise."

"I don't know if it will work," Jill said, but she looked as if she was seriously considering my proposal. I just needed one final push.

"And come on, it's extra backup for you. If Amanda gets all

dramatic and quits, you still have a Juliet. And I'm practically Amanda's size. I'll even fit into the costume. This is a win-win. Make me the understudy, please?" I folded my hands together and got down on my knees. "Please, please, please, please, please, please."

"All right, all right," she said. "Get up. I'll do it."

I jumped to my feet and pulled her into a big bear hug. "You are the best friend ever. Thank you so much. You won't regret this."

I could tell she thought this plan was out there, but I knew it would work! It was the perfect scenario and so much better than being the real Juliet. I was going to be able to sit in on every rehearsal, get close to Romeo, and never have to take the stage. My plan to win over Wes was officially under way!

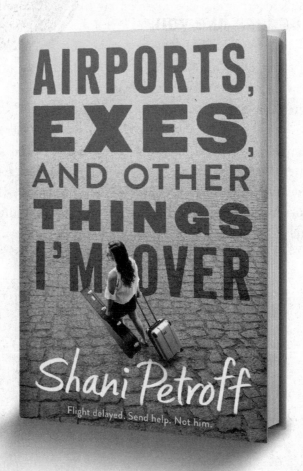